Big Bones Don't Break

We Just Have More to Love Part II

W. ROGER BROWNLEE

COVER MODELS:
JESSICA WILLIAMS (FRONT COVER),
EBONI MUSE (FRONT COVER IN RED)

DEDICATED

Once again to those

who call themselves

Big and Beautiful

ACKNOWLEDGMENTS

First, I give thanks to Our Heavenly Father by way of Jesus. To Mom, thank you, for the many years you struggled and gave selflessly.

To my son Isaiah, the day you came into my life my whole world changed. Even though you are so young, you have taught me so much. I can hope and pray that, I can be the teacher and mentor you need me to be. To Kevin Luna, I am so proud of you! Make your mark in this world...claim your immortality. I LOVE YOU BOTH!

My dear friend Jennifer Lynn Wells, words can never express how grateful I am to have you in my life. Carlows, (Carlos) I can always depend on you to come through, know that *"I always got your back!"* Johnny Lassiter & Kevin Walker, you two have been like and are consider family, brothers to this end. NISH!

Omayra Murray, you and I go back to when 50 Cent was asking *"21 Questions."* I have always admired your strong persona, so much that, I created a character in your honor (*Ivete Morales*). To Bonita Snow, Tonya Blackson, Teresa Bryant and Lisa Wright, without you this book would just be a bunch of words. Much Thanks!

Special thanks to Carolyn Smith Clark, Charlene Veney, Cathy Neal, Charade Estes, Danita Coleman, Reanne Richards, Carretta Smith, Herb Hunter, Author-Ramona Adkins and Thredda Sanders.

And to love much Brownlee Family in the DC Metro Area, Greenville & Spartanburg, SC, Memphis, TN, Locust Grove, GA, Chicago, IL and nationwide.

A real man cares about the size of your heart
Not the sizes of your dress.
~~author unknown

CHRISTINA & JAMES

Since that faithful day China Peoples came into Christina Jones' life her it has done a complete 3-60. Four years have passed; she is engaged to be married and has her own real estate business. Things were going well for her until nine months ago when her fiancé James lost his job as a cable TV installer.

You see, one of his girlfriends filed a sexual harassment complaint against him, the moment he refused to give her additional premium channels after he illegally connected her cable.

The results of the company's investigation were unfounded, primarily because she did not want to explain, how he got a key to her apartment, so the company opted to terminate him for unauthorized connection of service due to the lack of information.

Based on this event, their engagement ended up being put on hold, but we all think she should leave him alone and move on. Since that day, he has yet to find a job, although it would help if he were actually looking for one. God knows, the additional income would lighten the load off Christina's shoulders. It is hard enough for her to pay the bills in addition to planning a wedding and James' reckless spending habits does not help one bit.

The best decision she made was to start putting a little money aside from the rental of her grandfather's house. No one, not even I had any idea the real estate market would come to a screeching halt the way it did, if she did not take those precautions, there is no telling where they would be right now.

One day, Christina hauled her curvaceous size twenty-two physique home, seeking tranquility from the anarchy of the day's hustle. As she crossed through the doorway of her humble home, her anger shot through the roof.

Once again, she found her place in worse shape than it was when she rushed out early just in time to catch the D58 bus. Cigarette butts from the last twelve hours seemed to spill over from a nearby ashtray and the disgusting stench of tobacco and weed seemed to secrete from the walls of her living room.

She made her way passed the numerous empty liquor and beer bottles that concealed her coffee table on her way to the kitchen. She became more infuriated, to find all the dishes from the morning's meal she speedily wash before leaving out, barely in time to catch her bus, seem to be restored and increased two-fold.

"This man has been home all day and hasn't done a damn thing," she said repulsed by his trifling regard for their home. "I suppose, I am expecting too much to think he would pick me up from my job at least one day out of the month, after all he is driving my car."

She placed her things on the dining room table and headed back to her bedroom. She sought a moment before tackling the laborious task of putting her house back in order.

Her moment of peace was abruptly interrupted by a wet sensation on her back as she lay on the bed.

She sat up to investigate, "What is so soggy that it could seep through my bra and blouse?" she asked. "This lazy man can't do anything right!" She declared assuming he left a damp washcloth on the bed, but shocked to discover the wet spot was so immense it soaked through sheets down to the mattress.

"What is this?" She looks closer, feeling the texture and smelling a familiar scent. She thinks, but cannot seem to connect the scent to a source. She sniffs and sniffs until the smell hits her, dropping the sheets, "I can't believe this no good man has screwed some slut in my bed!"

Anger, combined with anguish and misery, overwhelms her entire body. She rushed to the phone to call her best friend Ivete.

Ivete Morales has been her best friend, since the first day they met as freshmen in high school. At age 14, Ivete moved to the area from Chicago and did not know anyone at the school. Only by faith, she happened to pass by as four senior girls were tormenting and teasing Christina.

"Hey, look its Miss Piggy, here piggy, piggy, piggy!" they called out.

Ivete always had a soft spot in her heart for the underdog, being one of six Puerto Ricans in her last school; she always dealt with teasing by other girls for being different. Upon hearing the girls' disrespectful rants, she without a second thought came to Christina's rescue.

Dropping her books, she rushed over to stand in between Christina and her harassers, took off her bamboo earrings, assumed a boxer's stance, and prepared for battle. "If you Hoes got a problem with her, then I got a problem with you," she said with conviction.

It was obvious the girls did not want any part of Ivete, because they quickly walked away. After the threat was neutralized, Ivete turned to Christina, fixed her clothes, wiped the tears from her eyes, and walked her to class. "Don't worry about those cunts, Sweetie. I let them bitches know, I am the Queen Bitch around here, and they won't bother you again. But if they do, I gots something for that ass!"

Ivete answered and, Christina went straight to the point no warm greeting, just stickily business, "Girl, This man done brought one of them Tricks up in my house and screwed her in my bed."

Upon hearing, the latest incident between James and Christina, Ivete went ballistic, "Oh, hell naw, that Negro lost his mind? Am I gonna need to bust a cap in his punk ass?" Ivete brought up the same statement she had made many times before, "Chris, I keep telling you he ain't no fucking good and you needed to leave his fucking ass a long time ago." Then she asked, "Have you told China about this yet?"

Ivete and China have not known each other long, they met through Christina, because Ivete sees China holds Christina's best interest in heart they all are very close.

"No, I called you first."

"Get her ass on the phone, maybe she can talk some sense into your hard-headed ass."

"OK hold on, let me switch over," Christina switches over and dials China

China answers, "Hello?"

"Hey girl, its Chris and Ivete is on the other line."

"What's good China?" Ivete says.

"Oh, hey Vette."

"Chris, go ahead and tell China what your weak ass excuse of a man did, go on tell her….tell her."

Just as Christina began to speak, Ivete jumps in, "That sorry worthless piece of baboon shit brought some crack-head up in her house and fucked the slut in her bed."

China stunned to hear this, "Oh my God, Chris please tell me you didn't walk in while they were going at it."

"No, I found a big wet spot in my bed; his vile ass didn't have the sense or the decency to change the sheets."

China lets out a big groan, "James needs his ass whipped!"

"Thanks China, that's exactly what I want to do to him," Ivete declared.

China laughs in assurance, "Girl, I'm sure what you want to do involves knives, matches, gasoline and someone facing gun charges."

"And, what is the problem with that?" Ivete asks.

China has always been the voice of reason amongst the group, "Well, I for one don't want to be in court testifying for your crazy ass again" Slightly embarrassed Ivete finds this amusing and laughs, as China continues, "Do you always solve your problems with random acts of extreme violence?"

"Child please! What I want to do will not be random. I will make sure it is specific, detailed and very carefully carried out. You can believe me on this shit!" Ivete professed.

"Vette, this type of situation requires rational thinking and tact."

Ivete still being Ivete, "Yeah, tact, like cutting off his dick and tacking his shit to a refrigerator like a magnet. China, you can sit there all you want and try to tell me there is a better way to handle this. But you know damn well, if Nee did this to you, you'd have his nuts cut off and they'd be dangling on your living room wall."

Protecting her man China replies, "No, I will never have to worry about Nee stepping out cause I make sure all his wants, needs, and desires are met to the fullest. In fact, I'm gonna take care of those needs as soon as he gets home and you can believe me on that."

Christina adds, "Yeah Ivete, I'm convinced also you need some help with your anger issues. Maybe you need a steady man in your life too."

This struck a nerve with Ivete, "Shit, I don't need a steady man! I can do everything myself."

China embellishes in a devilish tone, "Yeah, but it sure feels good to go to bed and wake up with one beside you. And I don't see how you can go so long without having a man around you, on you and yes Lawd, inside you."

Curiosity gets the best of Christina, and being they all are so close she asks. "Ivete, how do you manage when Bruce is gone so long? I mean, don't you get lonely and need to be touched? It's been about 2 or 3 years since you last seen Bruce and you should have at least a side piece by now."

"Shit! I got a boyfriend, his name is Victor."

Astonished, China and Christina both in unison say, "What?"

Ivete repeats and elaborated, "That's right, I got a man, and he handles my intimate needs, never gets tired and is ready whenever I am."

Doubting Ivete, China questions her further, "Vette, your man doesn't get tired?"

"Nope, I pop in 2 fresh batteries every month and Vibrating Victor is good to go."

Christina outraged and appalled, "Oh my God, Ivete, I can't believe you said that so openly."

"Chris, ignore this crazy heifer. There is no way you can substitute plastic for the hot hard body of a man." She continued with so much sensitivity and energy, "I'm sorry, but Vette is wrong, a cold piece of plastic can't give back the same type of vigor, passion, and touch like a man. Her voice changed to a soft yet sensual pitch, "Nor can a machine ever, feel as good as the hard, stiff, hot, and throbbing meat of a man when he is inside your wet moist kitty." She starts to fan herself, "In fact, I'm getting soaked thinking about Nee."

Christina cries out "Oh Girl, *TMI! TMI!*"

"Look, I gotta go get ready, my man will be home soon and I'm gonna give him the best welcome home present he has had in a long time." Then she switches back to the problem at hand, "Chris, I will support whatever you decide to do, but be sure you can live with your decision. And please don't let this Latina *Annie Oakley* talk you into doing something, which I would have to bring you cigarettes on visitor's day…okay? "

Christina answers, "Okay."

"Alright, I'll talk to y'all later."

China hangs up the phone as Ivete and Christina continue. "Girl, I told you from day one, to leave James' tired ass alone. But did you listen to me?"

"Well, in the beginning James was sweet and kind, I think it's because he is under a lot of stress from being laid off."

"Laid off? That's bullshit! Your dumb ass would believe anything he tells you. He's playing you Chris and you aren't smart enough to see."

This comment puzzled Christina, "What do you mean, playing me?"

"I bet he asked, when y'all first started to talk, what you were looking for in a man and you told him like a dumb ass."

"What's wrong with that? We were getting to know each other."

"Girl, don't you know this is the biggest mistake women make? The first thing a man wants to know is what we are looking for in a man. Once he knows all your dreams and desires, he uses this to get his crusty ass foot in the door. The next thing you know his trifling ass is sitting on your sofa. You will also notice that those same funky feet he used to tip-toe in your heart were propped up on your coffee table." This newly acquired knowledge amazes Christina, "Wow."

Not quite finished Ivete resumes, "Months pass and then you start to notice a change, but there is no real change. When he sees you're hooked, he drops the fake persona of being the man you have been looking for and reveals who he is. Then you are sitting there like a dumb ass wondering why he has changed. When he's hasn't changed at all, he's showing you the asshole he actually is."

"No not James, he has a lot on his mind. First, his mom kicks him out with no place to go. Then he got fired from one job, and another. How much can one person take?"

"Chris, this where you made your second mistake, when you told me he is 35 years old and still lives at home with his mom, I told you to leave his ass alone. Didn't I?"

"Yes, you did," Christina timidly she answers.

"And when you told me his mom kicked him out and he had no place to go. I told you not to let him move in with you. Didn't I?"

Now a little annoyed, "Yes Ivete, you did."

"I know I did, but you still let that sorry motherfucker move in…why?"

"Ivete, what is the real reason you don't like him?

This question provoked a quick response from Ivete, "How many times I gotta tell you? He ain't shit! He can't keep a job. He relies on you to support his ass and now he's screwing dirty ass floozies in your bed!"

Ivete held back hesitant to say, what weighed so heavy on her heart and mind, but feeling as strongly as she did about what her longtime friend has subjected herself to; she is compelled to say it. "For all you do for him; he repays you by cheating on you. And then when you confront him about what's going on he beats you?" Ashamed Christina drops her head.

Finally free from the heavy burden, Ivete continues, "Yeah, that's right I know about the bruises you try to cover up and I know good and well that black-eye you had a couple of months ago did not come from some damn door knob."

Christina head drops even lower for the truth has a very bitter taste.

"You wanna know what totally fucks my head up Chris…huh? Ivete asks, Is how you let this man, no wait, I'm gonna call him exactly what he is."

Chris could hear the disappointment in Ivete's voice as she continued, "You let this boy take something from you no man can give you. You let him take your pride and self-respect. Sweetie, when he hurts you he is also hurting me?"

"How so?" Christina asks.

Ivete paused to gather her emotions "Chris, you are like family to me. Do you remember back in high school the first day we met?"

"Yes."

Ivete goes on, "To this day you think the first time we met was the day those girls tried to bully you, but it wasn't. The first time, actually we met was on the 2nd day of school during lunch."

Her tone switches to reveal her softer and gentler side, "I sat outside of the cafeteria. I didn't wanna go inside because I didn't have any money and you found out later my mom was so into her boyfriend and drugs she was hardly there. That's why my father took me from her before I graduated high school."

China's mouth dropped open as Ivete continued to open up, "We never had any food in our house, so it wasn't like I could bring lunch to school."

"Oh Ivete." Christina said touched by what her best friend shared.

"This one day in particular for some reason you came outside to eat, you saw me and you offered to share your lunch with me. Her emotions got the best of her causing her voice to crack, "Christina, I had not eaten a full meal in 2 days, but you gave me most of your food."

"I always made a big lunch." She joking said to lighten the mood.

"Yeah, I tried to cover it up, but your mom knew what was going on. That's why she allowed me to come over so many days for dinner and spend the night. I grew to love you both as the sister and real mom I never had."

In this moment of reflection, the seldom seen docile side of Ivete exposed itself to Christina. "Before my Poppy got me back, you and your mom were the only family I had and all my siblings are boys so you are the closest thing I have to a sister." Yet, the moment quickly ended when

Ivete's thoughts moved back on the subject of James. "And I be damned, if I let some no good bastard hurt my family.

Christina thinks for a moment, "Wait Vette? They don't have prayer in school."

"I know that's how much I don't like him. It will be over before I get started."

Christina hears James as he starts to enter the house. "Oh, he's here, I gotta go. So, we're still on for lunch tomorrow right?"

"Sweetie wait, you don't have to get off the phone because he came home."

"He'll get mad if he finds out I'm talking to you."

"Fuck him! After what he did in your house, in your bed, how dare he say anything to you about you being on the phone with anybody or me? Who in the hell do he think he is?"

James walks in and immediately comes over to Christina, "Who the fuck are you talking to?"

Christina quickly hangs up before he could get any closer.

"Who were you talking to Christina?"

She timidly responds, "Oh, no one important."

He becomes a little agitated, "I said, who in the fuck, were you talking to?

She repeats, "No one important."

He got in her face, "I'm gonna ask your fat ass one more damn time and you better answer me. Who the hell were you talking to?"

She finally gives in, "I was talking to Ivete."

James goes ballistic, "How many fucking times, I got to tell you, I forbid you talking to her. I don't like her trouble-causing dyke ass. All she wants to do is fill you head up with a bunch of bullshit."

"James, she's not like that, she my best friend and she's not gay."

"When we decided to get serious, I was supposed to become your best friend and you were to cut her off."

Christina tried to defend her friend, "Well, she says men come and go, but your friends are there for you until the very end."

"I don't give a damn what her man hating ass says. If you ask me, I think that bitch is a dyke and wants you for herself."

"But no one asked you." She mumbles with malice yet it was not low enough he heard every word.

"What the fuck did your fat ass say? He clenched his fists and moved closer, "So talking to her, got you feeling a little brave.... huh?"

She did not answer, so he moved even closer grabbing and yanking her hair back. "You back talking me, bitch?"

"No James, I wasn't."

"Oh, I thought not." Lessening his grip, "So, what you cook to eat?"

"I have not started dinner yet."

"Hold up, you been home all this time and you ain't cooked my dinner? You'd rather spend all your time talking on the phone to bull dagger girls, instead of taking care of your man...huh?

"No."

"Now, what the fuck was y'all talking about that took all of your attention away from making sure all my needs are met?"

She summoned up enough courage to break away from his vice like grip, "I was telling her about the cum stains you and one of your other women left in my bed"

"What?"

Now with a lot more confidence, "I said, I was telling her about the cum stain, you made screwing one of your nasty hoes in my bed."

First at a loss for words, then finding them he asked, "What are you talking about?"

"So you don't know what I'm talking about …huh James?" She rushes into her bedroom, snatches the sheets off the bed, and then throws it at his feet.

"Then what in the hell is this?"

Even though caught red-hand, he relied on the lessons he learned reading the International Playas Handbook. Sadly, this is the only book he ever read cover to cover. He recalls.

Chapter 7, Section 5

When your woman catches you cheating, use the PDS method:

"P" Play Dumb-

I don't care if you have multiple degrees if you want to get out of hot water with your woman you must act like you have a 2nd grade education. Act as if you do not know anything about what they have found or discovered.

"D" Deny Everything-

There are certain answers to questions she still has not discovered. If you deny everything, it will force her to reveal all she knows or thinks she knows. Therefore, you do not supply additional information that will get you caught up.

"S" Switch the Blame-

Find something about the situation to reverse the fault back in her direction. Accuse her of not having faith or trusting you. Trust or lack of it can be your best weapon using this system.

This tactic is similar to the Jedi Mind Trick from the Star Wars Movies. Use trust against her like, Darth Vader used the dark side of the Force to dominate, the first three movies in the Star Wars Episodes. This has been used many times over and proven to work 9 out of 10 times.

Use the Force and use it well, Padawan (My Jedi Apprentice).

James tries the PDS method, "I don't know what the hell you are talking about. It's not mine and why the fuck are you asking me about your sheet. I need to be asking you the same thing" She folded her arms not believing him, "James, don't try to play dumb." Playing it dumb and denying it failed. "Why the fuck are you checking up on me? I'm a grown ass man. Don't you think, if I wanted to sleep with someone, I would do it somewhere else than here?"

He then put the third method into play. "So, that's how it is now you don't trust me. After all the time we spent together, where is the trust in our relationship. OK Christina, if this is how things are now, then I'm out!"

He walked passed gathering his things, which should not have taken as long as it did to pack six items.

James did not give her a second to think clearly, he took advantage of her emotional uncertainty, "When I'm gone, you're gonna realize how good you had it with me. I mean look at you! While pointing at her, "Do you think anybody else is going to find your sloppy fat ass attractive? No man wants a woman who is the same size as a grizzly bear."

He had some nerve to say such barbarous things like to her. He was not even close to being a prize himself. He was 5-foot-4 and a frail looking 109-pound, pygmy with no job. The only reason the other women hang out with him is because, he always bought the weed they smoke.

He really wasn't going to leave her, because he knew if there is no Christina, there is no money, and if, no money then no liquor or weed therefore no more women. Thus, his plan was to destroy her self-esteem so she would think if she lets him go, she would spend another 5-10 years alone without a man.

As he predicted she took every word he said to heart, she gave in, "James, I'm sorry please don't leave!"

His back to her, he smirks realizing his trick worked. If it were anyone else they would have been humbled and apologize for their part in the situation, but not James. "Why should I, if you don't trust me and keep accusing me of cheating on you?"

"So, where did the wet spot in the sheet come from, James?"

Still not willing to admit his wrongdoing, "It didn't come from me."

"Then, where did it come from? It was not present when I got out of bed this morning and it did not come from us, because you have not touched me in over a month."

"Maybe one of your girls brought a man over here and had sex in your bed. I bet it was your carpet-munching girlfriend Ivete, evil bitch always trying to set me up like Marion Barry at the Vista Hotel. In fact I thought I saw her car parked outside around lunch time"

She could not believe that he would come up with some implausible lie like that. Ivete had been at her desk all day, in fact she had to be dragged away to go to lunch. James was as bad at lying as he was at cheating. I cannot believe she fell for his lame ass lie but she did so I guess James will be around for a while.

Clear across town Ivete knew by the abrupt end of the discussion Christina would give in and take James back. This infuriated her, so she needed to blow off some steam. Blowing of steam to you or I would be something like going to a bar or club for drinks, or even taking a long drive. Ivete on the other hand, her idea of blowing off steam is going to the pistol range and firing a hundred rounds downrange

She loaded a magazine to her sliver plated .40 caliber Glock, then fired until the gun emptied, "That's right James, keep fucking over my girl, your days are numbered you bastard."

NEHEMIAH & CHINA

It was about 6 months before Nee and China's big wedding day and when they decided to move in together. This was a very easy transition to make as they were always together anyway, for he would always sleep over at her place or vice versa. They have been together for close to a decade and inseparable.

It was about 6pm, when Nee came through the front door. Not a single light was on in the apartment. It appears that no one was home. This was very odd; China was always waiting with a warm loving welcome.

Cautiously he closes the door behind him and continues in.

"What the?" puzzled by the darkness of his apartment. "Why are all of the lights off and where is China?

His senses heightened with every step he took deeper into the abyss. Every sound seemed to radiate becoming clearer and sharp as a razor's edge. His ears locked in on, the faint but sweet and familiar sound of Duke Ellington & John Coltrane's "In a Sentimental Mood" coming from behind his bedroom door. The dim light from behind the door crept out from under it and tiptoed alongside the scented melody that enticed him to come closer.

At the door, he warily opened to look inside. Then a voice summoned him. "Come in and strip."

He recognized that it was China, "What?"

"You heard me, I said strip. Take off all your clothes." China commanded as she stood in the doorway of their bathroom, wrapped in a towel.

Still puzzled, "What, huh?"

"Look Negro, either you take off all your clothes, or I will take them off for you. But, I'm warning you if I take them off. I'm not going to lay them down neatly, like you do. Where they lay is where they're gonna stay."

Still somewhat bewildered and not knowing what to make of what was going on.

"Huh?"

"Come on Baby? You're spoiling the mood."

At times, Nee is about as quick as catching hints as an ice cube melting during a snowstorm.

"What mood?"

China took a step closer and drops the towel from her body, revealing all of her glory before him. The sight of her voluptuous body abducted Nee's mind, holding it for ransom and the only payoff would be

China left in ecstasy.

She moved even closer, "If you see something you like, don't hesitate to grab it."

His eyes skimmed hungrily up her body, as it tapered out from her size 8 feet, then widened up from her calves that were the size of ripe grapefruits and expanded at her knees.

It arched out at her thighs and expanded to the full 65 inches of her hips, then pitched back into a 49-inch waist, and finally back out to her 44DD breast.

Her body kinda reminded him of a Bass Cello, and he wanted to pluck all her strings. He then chuckles thinking to himself, "If she keeps this up, she will definitely be hitting some high notes tonight."

His eye then continued up to her full, but pouty lips recalling the last time they met his. When his deep-set eyes met her slanted eyes, they zeroed in and locked with no deviation, not even to blink.

So much was being said, yet not a word was spoken. This gave China great delight, to see that her seductive hints were received well, so she took her flirting up a notch. She completely turns around so he could get a full rear view.

Giggling and in a childlike voice, "Oops, I dropped my towel." then bends over exposing all of her bountifulness.

It was at that moment, Nee began to quick rip off his clothes, and for once, it didn't matter where they landed. Normally he would have taken the time to neatly fold them and put them aside.

This time, he didn't care where they went; he had bigger and better things on his mind.

He grabbed her by the arm then turned her around, so they were facing each other.

"Come here you!"

Her face lit up in delight of being in his arms so, that she held onto him as though her life depended on it. This moment was topped off by deep and passion kisses. All systems go; she took this as a green light to carry out her well thought out plan.

As they broke from their kiss, she led him into their bathroom. The illumination of the light from the candles, bounced from wall to wall giving the right amount of its soft radiance to solidify the ambiance, she worked diligently to prepare.

In the tub were red and yellow rose pedals. Yellow symbolized their eternal friendship, having been best friend for many, many years and sharing countless trials and tribulations together. Red was symbolic of his undying love for her, believing that God made her only for him.

An oil burner slowly simmered releasing the sweet nectar of frankincense that had such an addictive quality; Nee could not avoid being pulled in by its delicious flavor.

She chose this as a representation of his essence. Like the frankincense, it was sweet, flavorful, and intoxicating. He inhaled its bouquet as she drew in his spirit, making her yearn for him more and more.

She climbed into the tub and he quickly followed her. She rested her body against his, letting the ambiance further establish the mood.

22

"Wow, you really know how to make a man feel special."

"Well Baby, how are you feeling right now, is exactly how you make me feel every day." She said as he held her tighter and tighter as they seemed to melt sinking deeper and deep into the bubbles.

An hour later, they exited the tub. Nee existed first grabbing a nearby towel and with total disregard to himself, he began to blot dry China's body.

Once every droplet was blotted from her body, he began to tend to his body. China being attentive promptly assisted.

They both strolled into the bedroom, where China slowly crawled to the center of the bed. Nee grabbed a bottle of oil then joined her.

"Turn over" he gently whispered.

Without hesitation she turned over onto her stomach then, he mounted her. In position, he tilts the bottle letting little droplets of oil pour out. Each drop that met her skin seemed to be frigid and cold that she trembled in anticipation of the next.

The mild and tenderness of his hands eradicated the mischievousness as they modestly manipulated the oil droplets into her skin. Euphoria made, her eyes roll back into her head as his touch provoked Goosebumps to erupt all over her body.

She knew he was good with his hands, so she prepared herself for the worst. His hands lightly and delicately surfed from her shoulder blades down to the center of her spine then to her bottom.

"Oh shit!" ripped from her lips as his hands grabbed each of her cheeks clutching them with a vise like grip.

He then, skillfully raked his nails along the back of her legs down to her knees.

"Oh damn!" as she rose up off the bed not able to control her body's reaction to the feeling his nails gave her.

At her ankles his hands moved to the inside of her legs then, swiftly pulled them apart, instantly her level of arousal shot up 10 degrees.

"That's right Baby, take it." She said in her head, wanting him to devour her right then and there.

Although, it did cross his mind to get down to business, Nee had other things in mind, as he poured more oil onto her. His hands continued to rub oil between her thighs a little below her Sweetness then out to her hips.

He paused a moment, to gaze at all her generously proportioned body in awe. He had no idea 11 years ago all that this would be his. Nor did he even imagine that this voluptuous woman would be someone that he'd hunger to be near her every minute they were apart.

Prior to the two becoming a couple, he never found women of size attractive. He always went after women half her size. Yet, now he sees her, and women like her equally beautiful.

They say that a leopard can't change its spots, and that is true but leopards can change their prey. Moreover, tonight he was the hunter and she was his prey.

He suddenly stopped, concerned and a bit puzzled she looks back at him, "What's wrong why did you stop?"

"Nothing, hold that thought." He says as he gets up and head towards the kitchen.

From the kitchen, she hears a series of beeps from the microwave, "I know he didn't stop, to go get something to eat just as things were getting started?" she asked.

He reentered the room and assumed a position beside her on the bed. She rose up off the pillow when she hears a snapping noise.

Trusting him fully, she relaxed laid back down; this was one of the fruits of being best friends for 11 years before becoming a couple, the trust never died it only became stronger.

She arches her back, as he slowly poured warm honey down the center of her spine from her shoulder blades down to her waist. It was hot enough to cause her whole body to quiver and shake uncontrollably.

He continued to pour the honey down her back once reaching her cheeks making sure that each cheek received its equal share.

"Oh my God, Boy, what are you trying to do to me?"

He answered in a soft but rich voice, "I'm only trying to love you the way you deserve to be loved Sweetheart."

Resuming the task at hand, he applied more of the sugary mixture down each of her legs, applying just enough so it would flow down to the side yet, not run on to the bed.

"So my love, are you ready?" he asked.

Without haste she answered, "Yes Baby, I am so ready."

He then began to feast on her honey glazed bronzed cheeks. Her back arched from the pleasant and almost unbearable intensity of his warm wet tongue as he sucked up the bee's sweet nectar along with a nice healthy portion of her flesh.

The honey now gone from her plushy bottom, Nee didn't stop he poured a little more honey on her, this time letting it fall down between into the crack of her mountainous cheeks. He pauses for a moment allowing it to run down deep into her abyss.

China tightly clinches the bed sheets in anticipation of where he had to go to lick up the honey. It was a place no one has ever gone or ventured before. Yet, as always with Nee, there were many firsts and many surprises. One thing she had come to learn, always expect the unexpected.

And yes, sure enough she was right, Nee parted her love mounds, and plunged his face deep between her immense glistening derriere. He drove his face deeper and deeper until reaching his target.

When his tongue met her tightly puckered aperture, she clutched it tighter and tighter. China's response to this was strictly by impulse, the more his tongue made contact it seemed the more she pushed it back up at up to aid help him.

It seemed the more he pushed forward the more she pushed back, until she felt his tongue move up, down and around here tightly puckered fissure. She felt a pleasure that was unlike anything she has ever felt before; sending chills that shot throughout her body like a jolt of electricity.

It was so intense she bit down on her pillow so she could hold back a thunderous roar of "Oh shit!" That would be so loud that Mrs. Oates, three floors up would hear everything. The feeling teetered on a thin line between pleasure and toe curling. He sensed that she was a little thrown off by this so he asked, "Sweetheart, are you okay with this? Do you want me to stop?"

Fearful of it coming to an abrupt end, she grabbed each of her generously sized cheeks parting them further granting full and unrestricted access." Oh shit baby, don't stop! Please, don't stop. "She desperately pleaded with him.

Stopping was the farthest thing from his mind; he had no intentions on stopping. He was a man on a mission, one man with one goal in mind and that was to turn China's ass out. The more she pushed back the deeper he drove his face, only coming up to clutch a little bit of air before pressing forward.

China was taken to a higher level of ecstasy that she has never been to before. Her moans grew and swelled so loud that it ripped through the pillow and it was no way of avoiding it at this point. Ms. Oates was going to get an ear full of the *sex-capades* in the Nebo house tonight.

It was at that moment when China was removed from her blissful dream by a knock at the door. Gathering her senses then grabbing her bathrobe from a nearby chair, she proceeded to answer her door.

"Who is it? She reluctantly cried out.

27

Only to become extremely irritated to hear, "Girl Scouts would you like to buy some cookies?"

Her response when she opened the door was totally out of her character, but if you were suddenly robbed of the conclusion of a HOT and steamy dream. How would you have responded?

"No, I don't want your damn cookies! She slammed the door in the faces of the two adorable little girls adorn in their khaki uniforms.

Later, she will probably regret being so rude and harsh, but that would be much, much later. She would first have to get over the fact that the Girl Scouts cookie drive prevented her from getting a much-needed release.

She decided that since she was abruptly woken up, she'd make herself breakfast. We all know that once you wake up from a good dream you can't go back and pick up from where you left off.

A few minutes passed, before her phone rang.

"Hello, Oh hi Mommy."

Resuming her meal, "I know, it is too early to be up on a Saturday and I would still be sleep if those girl scouts hadn't awakened me up."

Her mother on the other end of the phone, "How is Nee?"

Hesitating before answering, "I don't know I have not spoken to him in about a week."

"Oh China, that does not sound like a happy bride to me. What's going on?"

"Nothing Mommy." She became a tad bit fidgety and her voice now a faint squeaky.

"You're lying!"

"Mommy everything is fine."

"China Symone, you forgot who you are talking to. I am your mother and I know you like I know myself and you're lying!"

"No Mommy, everything is fine."

"Now even firmer, "Little girl you are forgetting who you are talking to. After 27 years of nurturing you from the cradle through grade school and then through college, from your first crush to your first broken heart, I have been here for you and will continue to do the same, No matter what, but I can't help you get through tough times when you don't share your pain with me."

China finally breaks down, "Nee and I had a fight, and we're not talking."

Now she spoke in a more sympathetic tone, "Ah Baby, what happened?" She paused a moment in thought, "Please don't tell me he's still stuck on your size"

"No Mommy that's not it, all began when we started making plans for the wedding. Everything was going good until we started on the invitations."

"Oh, something like that can easily be overwhelming, but you both just need to compromise a little. So, I assume he wanted to invite that conceited ex of his and you don't want her to come.....right?"

"No Mommy, it's a little bit more serious than that."

"More, like what?"

China hesitated before continuing; she knew what she had to say was not going to be received well.

"Mommy, Nee says that if Janice comes he doesn't want her to sit with you on the front pew at the ceremony nor does he want her to sit at the family table during the reception. He wants her to sit with everyone else."

Having dealt with adversity for many years now, China's mother was no stranger to others objection to her chosen lifestyle. For it was a hard pill to swallow, especially for her ex-husband, China's father Ray.

It came out of nowhere and he was devastated when she told him that she had been cheating and wanted to leave him. Then add insult to injury by telling him that her other man was not a man but a woman.

The male ego is a very sensitive thing, the news hurt China's father so much that to this day he still doesn't want to see or even talk to her. But then again it's only been 2 years since the split.

He agreed to be in the wedding and give China away, only if he did not have to sit anywhere near his ex-wife Deborah. He even opted to sit with Nee's family at the church and at the reception. They say that time heals all wounds but for now, wounds are still open. It took some persuading, but he knows what happened between him and Deborah had nothing to do with his baby girl's special day.

Deborah continues comforting China, "Sweetheart, it's not that much of a problem for us, Janice and I have walked down this road many times before.

We know that not everyone is accepting of our type of relationship. I'll talk to Janice, I'm sure she will see the big picture and will agree to this small condition."

"But Mommy that's not fair to Janice. She is just as much a part of my family as you and Daddy and she should be able to sit with the family."

"Baby, she loves you just the same, I'm sure she would not mind. We encounter this type of stuff all the time. Not everyone is open to our lifestyle."

Offering a little more to support her point, "And besides maybe its best that she doesn't sit with the family. You know your father still has not come to terms with me leaving him for her."

"Yeah, but Daddy needs to stop holding on to that and move on. If he could not find happiness with you then he needs to find someone else who will give him all that he needs."

"Wait, are we talking about the same man? The same man who thinks that the whole world should think like him?"

China a little leery, "Well, he can't keep holding on to a love that once was, even though it was a shock to everyone."

Deborah wanted to be sure that the blame of her failed marriage was divided equally, "A shock is an understatement! Baby let me tell you the truth about your father."

"Your father and I ended a long time ago; we just hid it from you."

"What do you mean; it ended a long time ago?"

"Sweetheart, I have been keeping this from you for a while and now that you're about to move forward with a new life. I think you should know the truth about your father."

What do you mean Mommy?"

"Baby, your father and I ended a long time ago. We just stayed together for your sake."

"No Mommy, Daddy told me that you were seeing Janice for some time before you two separated."

"Oh, is that what he told you?"

Her face now a little twisted, "Well, did he also tell you about the time I caught him in bed with Virginia?"

"Virginia, Daddy's secretary Virginia Mommy, no!"

"Yes, China that very Virginia and a few more before her and some more that have not been revealed yet."

China could not believe what she was hearing. The man who she thought was a loyal and dedicated husband turned out to be not so loyal.

Deborah continued to run down the list of the women that Ray cheated on her with.

"Let's see he had Madison, Frankie, and Celeste. Oh and then there was Chang who was Chinese, Lourdes from Panama, Tessima from Ethiopia, Irma from Germany and Trina from the hood."

"Mommy, you don't mean Trina from Oak Bridge Gardens do you?"

Some might say that your father did not discriminate. I say that he was just plain nasty."

China still shocked, "Is that the same Trina from Oak Bridge Gardens with the five bad ass kids?"

"Yeah, why your father went to a ghetto hood-rat half his age I have no idea. But, that is when I knew that it was time for me to move on.

China repeats, "Trina from Oak Bridge Gardens? Nee went out with her and almost got a beat down from some girl who she owed money to."

"Baby, when I found out the first time it really hurt me. I thought that your father was a good honest man, but that is far from the truth. He is just like all the other men out here. No damn good."

"Wow and all this time I thought that you just had a change of heart."

"No, I had no intentions of being with anyone. My goal was just to find someone to hang out with and before I knew it, Janice and I were really starting to hit it off. Then I started to develop feelings for her and before I knew it we were in bed together."

"Mommy, that's a little too much information."

Laughing, "Baby, you know me I don't like to keep any secrets from you?"

"True Mommy, but it's never too late to start." She joked.

They both laughed then Deborah said, "Baby, if you really want your marriage to last, you've got to pick and choose your battles. Some things are worth fighting for and some are not." China took this advice to heart as her mother went on, "Baby, you need to call Nee and make up with him. Don't let something like this ruin what is meant to be. I understand your loyalty to your family, but you are about to marry Nee. Once you say I do, he becomes your family and that is where your loyalty should be, with him."

"Yeah, I know but."

She then cut her off, "China, Janice, and I will always be here for you no matter what, but you need to follow your heart. You call him and make up now, so the next time we talk I want to hear that the things are okay and not the wedding is canceled. Do you understand me?"

Reluctantly, "Yes Mommy."

"Good, so talk to you later. I love you Baby, Goodbye."

"I love you too Mommy Goodbye."

RESOLVE & GROWTH

It was a very long day for Christina so; she decided to call it quits for the day. She began her pilgrimage home seeking refuge from the chaotic world of the real estate business.

Her feet were so swollen; it felt as if, with every step she took they were going to burst. Her day was completely consumed by showing house after house to the Vanderbilt's aka Mr. and Mrs. Indecisive. Who seemed to bicker over every property they viewed, but never agreeing on one.

They were her least favorite clients, for that last year now, every house he liked, and it appeared the venomous Zoe Vanderbilt always found that it was not acceptable for some reason or another.

Something as insignificant as the address displayed as words rather than numbers was enough to call off all prospects for that property. Does it really matter if the house's address displayed as Fifteen Twenty-two rather than 1522?

Although, Jonathan Vanderbilt was not any better he passed a nice house because he didn't like the color of the walls. Christina thought that with all the money he made, painting would not be an issue. Yet, she was wrong, if birds of a feather flock together, then Vanderbilt's are two old crows from the same cornfield.

Exiting off the bus, all she needed to do was to walk three more blocks and she was in the sanctuary of her home. For a few moments, the fantasy of James pulling up in the next car that drove by popped into her head.

However, that was about as conceivable as Osama bin Laden being invited to Sunday dinner at the White House. It was totally unlike James to be that thoughtful, so the dream quickly left her head just as quickly as it entered.

Just as she approached her house, she saw her car in the driveway and was somewhat shocked that he was even home. Although, this was somewhat odd, she did not give it that much attention so she opened the door and walked in.

"Lord Jesus, am I in the right house?"

She looked around and the house was impeccable. The house was in better order than it was when she ran out that morning.

"Now, this is more like it." Taking joy in a job well done, "This is what I'm talking about, I should be able to come home and just relax and not have to worry about doing anything but what to cook for dinner."

Reveling in the moment, she sat down on her sofa taking off her shoes then propping her feet up on the coffee table. For once, her thoughts were only about herself, even though James was somewhere in the house. It did not matter at that moment as she reclined, closed her eyes and slowly let the cushions of her sofa filter all of the day's stress from her body.

A faint moan of a woman suddenly ousted from her blissful state. This alarmed her slightly that she listened for another, but did not hear anything. Discarding it, she resumed her much needed moment of leisure, but in the back of her mind she knew that it would end and she would have to get up and start dinner.

Just then, she heard another moan, but this time it was louder and very conspicuously coming from her bedroom.

"Hmm, he must be looking at those nasty movies again." Closing her eyes once more struggling to find that harmonious zone of which the weird noise interrupted.

Suddenly, another moan followed by a thunderous thump against the wall and then someone screamed out the words "Oh shit." Unlike before this time it was clear and apparent, that the noises were coming from her bedroom.

Christina's heart felt like it dropped down into her stomach and her hands became clammy as she rose up from her resting place. With every step she took toward her bedroom, the sounds became clearer. Her heart began to beat like a jackhammer, apprehensive of uncovering what was so painfully obvious.

By the time she arrived at the bedroom door, her blood pumped throughout her veins with such ferocity it was like throwing a match into a barrel of gasoline. Preparing for war, she grabbed a broom on her way back.

Before she could turn the doorknob she heard, "Oh yes James, fuck this pussy— fuck this pussy."

When she heard this, she could not move terrified by what lied beyond the door. It was something on the other side she knew deep down to her inner core she could not bear. Therefore, she slowly and softly tiptoed back toward the living room.

"James, I think someone is out there," the female voice muttered.

Then the door swiftly opened and out walked James about as naked as Adam on the sixth day of Creation.

Surprised by Christina's presence, "What the hell you doing home so early?

She stopped dead in her tracks took a deep breath summoning up enough courage then turned around.

"How dare you, screwing another woman in my bed and in my house?"

"Fuck, it's my house too." was his response.

"No, this is my house and I let you stay here."

Just then the female exited the room, "Baby, what's going on out here and who the fuck is this hoe?"

This took Christina over the top, "Hoe? I got your hoe right here, Bitch."

She lunged at the girl grabbing a handful of her hair with her left hand and her right hand followed with uppercut after uppercut. Now the two locked up in combat, until James pulled them apart.

The girl turned to James, "You just let this busted freak come up in your house and attack me like this?"

Christina quickly corrected her, "No, hoe you got it all wrong, this is my house and I'm running shit up in here."

James turned toward the girl escorting her by the arm "Go in the room and get dressed, I got this."

The girl dumbfounded answered back, "But I."

He violently shoved her into the room cut her off before she could finish, "Did you hear me bitch, I said go in the room and get your shit, then get the fuck out. I told you I got this."

"That right skank, you heard him, get your shit and get out my house."

James then turned facing Christina, "So now you're checking up on me now huh? Your motherfucking ass is not supposed to be home this early."

This made her face become twisted, "What the hell has that got to do with you screwing some slut in my bed?"

He avoided answering her, "What? I suppose that dike Ivete put you up to some bullshit like this, didn't she?"

She didn't have to but Christina answered anyway, "No, I had a long day and my feet started to swell so I called it a day."

"See I told you that your fat ass need to go on a diet. Lugging around all that dead weight ain't good for you. Now your feet are big just like your ass."

This didn't deter Christina from the real issue at hand. She quickly got to the point, picking up the broom from the floor then clinching it, so tight her knuckle turned red.

"Negro, have you lost your mind bringing some loose huzzy in my house and hump her in my bed? Then you're gonna try to turn it around on me like it's my fault for coming home early."

Before he could answer the girl came out the room gave James a kiss, "Baby, call me later."

Christina could not believe that she had the audacity to do it in right in front of her. But, she was not going to let it go.

Grabbing the girl by her hair again, "I thought I told your tricking ass to get the fuck out my house."

James came to the girl's rescue once more breaking Christina's vise grip from the girl's head once more.

"Destiny, go ahead and get home, I'll give you a call later okay Beautiful."

Christina was taken back for a moment by the way James referred to Destiny; it was something that was similar to how he used to talk to her. This was something that left and has been absent from their relationship for many months now.

Destiny now safe from another ambush from Christina, James directs all his attention toward her.

"Now Bitch, what the fuck is your problem putting your hands on my guest. Have you lost your damn mind?"

"No but I think you lost yours bringing that tramp up in here."

"He then quickly got in her face, "Look Bitch, you don't run shit up in here. I run this motherfucking house and I didn't like the fact that you disrespected me in front of my company. Don't let that shit happen again or I will put my foot to your ass."

He turned to head back into the bedroom and just when his back was completely turned Christina seized the moment. She cracked him over the head with the broom.

Which triggered instant retaliation from James, "You Crazy Bitch, you're really showing your ass today huh? Well I got something for that ass."

He swiftly backhanded her then followed with several blows to her face. Normally she would have just stood there holding her ground trying her best to deflect the barrage of punches he delivered, accepting all the blame for her contribution to the latest bout of drama. But, no not this time, he committed the ultimate No-No and should pay for his transgression.

She then knew why Ivete was so adamant, even offering to foot the bill for her to take a kickboxing class at the gym. It proved to be very beneficial; this time around, she was not the only one who would leave from the battle with wounds. She held her own quite well, even countering a few of his punches.

Nonetheless, the tides had turned in James's favor when the fight went from a standing toe-to-toe exchange to a ground and pound scuffle completely dominated by him

It was at that moment; Ivete showed up at the front door hearing the ruckus in its entirety from the front porch she used her key to open the door. As always just like in grade school, Ivete came to her best friend's aid.

Although unlike the many other times before it was obvious by the blood, dripping from James nose that Christina made a valiant effort to handle it on her own.

Ivete hastily reached into her purse grabbed her old friend Mr. Reliable. He was actually, her Glock Model 27, .40-caliber subcompact pistol. I'm sure every single woman can relate that there is always one guy, who just can't seem to comprehend three simple words; wait, no and stop, but Mr. Reliable seems to break the language barrier with the quickness.

Her eyes seemed to sparkle at the sight of the cold black steal that appeared to fit so perfect in her hand. She yielded it as though it was an extension of her body.

Creeping up and placing the barrel at James's temple, "You got 5 seconds to get up off my girl or else I'm gonna take this gun from your head and stick it up your sugary ass."

"Oh Christina, here comes your manly friend to save you." he said as he got up.

Having gone back and forth with her many a day trading insults Ivete fired back. "You got some nerve calling me manly. If anyone around here is trapped in the closet, it's you. A man with breast?"

She paused turning her attention to Christina, "Are you okay Sweetie?" then continuing. "Look at your punk ass, your fucking breast are bigger than mine." Then she began to fuss sporadically in Spanish, "That got damn sweet ass fagot, I still don't know what she see in you anyway."

Regaining her composure and catching her breathe, "James, get all your shit together and get out. I'm tired of you beating on me. I'm tired of your cheating. I'm tired of your lies."

Then with a little more fire, "I want you out my life."

James with arrogance, "Are you sure that's what you want?"

Ivete answered for her not giving her time to second-guess her decision or herself, "I tell you what James, let me find out that you're still here when I get back. I know some villainous Vatos from Columbia Heights that would love to show you why it's bad to hit women."

James didn't take too kindly to this threat.

But, Ivete continues, "Yeah and I know that at least two of them just got home from the State Pen, so I know they would love your candy ass."

Sensing that enough was enough Christina summoned for Ivete, "Come-on girl, I'm ready to go.

Therefore, the era of James and Christina came to an ended.

REGRESS OR PROGRESS

Four months had passed and Christina once again was single. Ivete would call just about every evening to check on her before tuning in for bed. She made it her personal responsibility to ensure that she didn't have any free time.

From watching her girls in their past relationships, she learned that too much free time made the mind wander. It might not sound so bad to you or me, but Ivete knew that letting the mind wander after a bad break up was not good. It would lead to Christina thinking about all the things that happened, might have happened and things that will never happen.

She knew the more time Christina spent alone doing nothing; the probability of calling James was more relevant. This was something that Ivete refused to allow to take place. Christina had made significant progress to become independent and she'd be damn if all the time and energy invested would be thrown out the window.

One day, China and Ivete were sitting talking at Ivete's place, "Damn Vette, it's been so long since I've been to the gym. Maybe the next time y'all go, I'll go too." China said as she looked at herself in the mirror.

"Nah girl, you got too much on your plate already with your wedding. I don't think that now is a good time. Maybe after you get back from your honeymoon, then you could go." Ivete suggests.

"Yeah, I guess you're right"

"Oh, that reminds me I have to call my cousin to make sure she can pick you two up from the airport. Girl, you, and Nee are going to love P.R." Ivete said with pride.

"I hope so because this will be my first time leaving the country. Do I need to get a passport?"

"No Sweetie, if you are a US citizen you do not need a passport to go to Puerto Rico. Puerto Rico is part of the US, traveling to P.R. from the mainland is the same as driving from New York to Los Angeles."

"Oh Okay, I had no idea."

"Well I don't know about you, with those slanted eyes, you may have a hard time getting back in the country." Ivete uttered as she put her hands up to her eyes making them angle up to resemble an Asian.

"Ha-ha very funny." China sarcastically replies.

"Enough about P.R. Ivete changes the subject, "Have you seen Christina lately?

"No, why what's up?"

"Girl, our friend looks good since she lost 129 pounds."

China was a bit confused, "Wait, I thought you said she lost 20 pounds last week, where did the rest come from."

I know, she lost 20 pounds at the gym and dropped 89 pounds when she got rid of James's tired ass." Ivete answered.

"Girl you're crazy." China checked her watch, "Oh girl I gotta run, and I'm meeting Mommy for dinner."

"OK well, call me later. Okay?"

"I will and tell your mom, I said "Hi."

Later that day, Ivete stopped by Christina's house to pick her up for their weekly kickboxing class. When she got to the front door, she knocked several times, but no answer. This alarmed her; it was not like Christina not to answer the door.

She reached into her purse grabbing the spare set of keys Christina gave her just in case of an emergency. She slowly and stealthily opened the door. Her senses were in amplified.

Ivete was always ready for any confrontation and she always had her Mr. Reliable on standby. Her grandfather told her many stories of the victims he interviewed while he was a Chicago Police detective.

Women who lived alone were the prime targets for a home invasion. She vowed never to be a victim, so with *Mr. Reliable* her .40 caliber pistol at the ready she walked in the room.

She began a room-by-room search just as she had seen many times before watching all her favorite TV shows like Law & Order, Law & Order SVU, Law & Order Criminal Intent, and the many other Law & Order TV shows they have on TV these days. She started at the living room to the dining room to the kitchen and down the basement stairs. It was not until she reached the portion of the basement that lies just below Christina's bedroom when she heard a woman's voice upstairs.

She quickly dashed up the stairs headed to that room she mumbled, "That piece of shit James is screwing another bitch in my girl's bed again"

Just outside the door, she delicately pulled the slide back charging a round into the chamber of Mr. Reliable. Then, she kicked open the door and drew down and took aim on the large mass that was under the sheets.

"You sorry ass motherfucker, your days of doing my girl wrong is about to come to an end with the quickness." The large mass that was once moving on the bed froze.

"Show your face you sorry ass piece of shit. I want to see the fear in your eyes before I take your bitch ass out." She yelled out with pleasure. From under the sheets, James stuck his head out.

"What the fuck are you doing here, you crazy bitch?"

Ivete was so content having James in this compromising position, "I got your bitch right here, and this bitch has 16 rounds locked and loaded on your ass."

She noticed more movement from beneath the blanket, "Hey Hoe, I see you. You can come out from under blanket too."

Ivete was totally knocked for a loop when Christina peeked out from under the sheets then slid out from under James.

"Aw hell no." Ivete said as she lowered her gun. Her biggest fear had come true and the many weeks of struggling to help Christina regain her self-esteem went out the window with the dropping of James's pants. It took damn near an exorcism to expel the poisonous venom of detestation that James injected into Christina's mind the first time around.

"Chris, what in the hell are you doing getting back with this looser?" She said as she tried to overcome the jolt of this unpleasant discovery, "I was getting my freak on with my man until you rode in on your broom. But then again you haven't been with a man in so long; you would not know anything about that would you? James snidely answered.

Ivete quickly stuck her gun in his face then spoke through her teeth, "This is the second and last time I am gonna put my gun to your head. I swear on my grandfather's grave that if I have to do this again your ass is fucking done."

James did not surrender to her threats, "Fuck you bitch."

This took Ivete over the top; she took a step closer cocking back the hammer on Mr. Reliable, "Say one more word and I'll take your ass out right here and now. Say something, please say something." she begged and pleaded with him.

James being the asshole that he is, called her bluff and began to speak, but Christina stepped in between them to keep them separated. "You two stop it now."

She then turned to James, "Why don't you go get in the shower and let me handle this."

"Okay." He said as he walked out the room and passed Ivete, lunging at her trying to make her jump in fear. He had no idea that he was messing with the wrong person because she didn't even blink.

She just stood there with a cold hard stare looking him square in his eyes as she tightened the grip on Mr. Reliable even tighter than before.

Ivete is very dangerous when provoked, when she is pushed too far she has no boundaries. Growing up the youngest child of eight and only girl on the south side of Chicago, everything she needed she had to scratch, kick, or fight to get it.

Her father and older brothers made it their job to be sure their baby sister was a survivor. The three most important things they taught her.

1) To stand up for what you believe in.

2) Don't back-down from anyone and

3) To always look out for your love ones.

Family was the one thing they had and it was treasured dearly. If one sibling got into a jam, you could best believe the remaining seven would be there to aid. Ivete did not have a single worry in the world because they would give their lives for her.

They always said that she looked and acted just like their deceased mother even though she was their half-sister. So, if Ivete asked for the world on Sunday. Early Monday morning it would be on her doorstep.

Tony (53) and Isaac (52) the two eldest were defense lawyers in L.A. Paul (50) and David (47) were Chicago Police detectives following in the footsteps of their father and grandfather. Jacob and Job (43) the twins were Marines serving their sixth tour in Afghanistan and the youngest brother was Aaron (39), well he never really said what he does for a living. All they know is that he travels to foreign countries just as a war is starting. It's never talked about, when they find out he's leaving they just show him love and wish him a safe return.

If Ivete ever got in a jam, she knew her brothers would rush to her side. Whether it was with the law or anything else, just as long as they knew she believed in what she was doing and she was defending herself. So James definitely was barking up the wrong tree.

With James out the room Christina faced off with Ivete, "What are you doing here?"

Puzzled, "What do you mean what am I doing here, it's Thursday and you know we go to our kickboxing class every Thursday at 5pm. But I should be asking you why in the hell is he here, Chris?"

She asked, as she released the magazine clip then pulled back the slide of Mr. Reliable to remove the round from his chamber then puts him back in her purse.

"After the bullshit, that sorry excuse of a man put you through a few months ago, you let him come back. Why?"

"Because he loves me." Christina replied.

"Girl, his dumb ass can't even spell love, let alone know what it means."

"No, that's where you're wrong I know he loves me."

"Chris please, that man will say I love you to anything that has a snatch and some big breasts."

"No this is different." Christina barks out in denial.

"Girl, I can't believe this, he's feeding you a bunch of bullshit, and you just eat it up." Ivete said as she made a lip smacking sound with her mouth.

Christine still in denial, "No, he means it this time."

"How can you even consider taking him back, after what he did to you a few months ago or have you forgotten? Please say you used protection."

Hesitantly Christina answered, "Ah, no we didn't."

"Oh my freaking God, Chris what the fuck are you thinking? I saw the girl you caught him with and she looked like a walking bag of pus. She was downright nasty; I mean really Chris, a crack head looks like a supermodel compared to her."

Christina's head lowered as she pondered this unwelcoming fact which was right on the money as Ivete continued, "You must be out of your mind, with all those dirty hoes he messes with, what if he gives you something? She paused for a moment to look Christina dead in her eyes, "And I don't mean a baby either."

"Oh, I didn't think about that." Christina quietly responds.

"No, you didn't think at all." Ivete quickly snapped back at her.

She then took a deep breath gathered her thoughts and said; "Listen Sweetie, I'm hard on you like this only because I care about you. You're my girl and I don't like anyone doing you wrong and I don't want anything to happen to you."

"I know, but I need James." Christina said attempting to get some sympathy from Ivete.

"Oh, that's bullshit Chris and you know it. You need James, like a daycare needs to hire a pedophile. He's no good and not good for you."

"But, he said he loves me and only me."

"Girl, he don't love you, he tells you that, so he can stay at your place rent free. He loves that he can drive your car. He loves the money you give him, but he doesn't love you. And, what about all those ghetto and trashy hoes he screws? Is that how he loves you, by doing other women?"

"You're jealous that I have a man and you don't aren't you?" Christina fires back.

"Come on Chris, you can't be serious why would I be jealous of you and that loser?"

This really struck a nerve with Christina. "Ya know what Ivete, I think you should leave."

"What?" Ivete said in complete astonishment that her best friend who was the closest thing she had to a sister, would kick her out of her house. She could not believe that Christina would choose James over her or any man. This was against their sisterhood pact. Ivete was the only person who accepted Christina unconditionally and was always there for her.

Yet, she was being put on the shelf for a drug smoking, womanizing abusive loser. How could one man have so much power over her that she would turn her back on her friend?

Christina reiterates, "You heard me since you can't respect my man, it's best that you leave and not come around here anymore."

"Are you fucking kidding me? stunned Ivete said. Chris, have you lost your damn mind? She paused for a moment, thinking she would come to her senses, "Okay, if that's the way you want it, I'm outta here."

Ivete didn't know which hurt more, being betrayed by someone to whom she has been a loyal and faithful friend or because she was losing the closest person, she had to a sister.

It was obvious that Christina chose to be with James, rather than have her as a friend. Her mind was so clouded by losing out to the love of James that it over shadowed the devastation of losing family. She gathered her pride and quickly left the house.

However, by the time she got to her car, the pain got the best of her. She broke down, her fiery Latino spirit reduced to a flicker flame by the teardrops that fell from her weeping eyes.

Almost a decade and a half of devotion, trust, and allegiance seem to have been stripped from her by a man that was less than a man. Ivete would not have taken it so hard if James was everything that her best friend needed in a man. But then again, if James was responsible, thoughtful and if he proved worthy of Christina's love then there would not be any friction between them. Hell, she would love him as a brother because she'd know that her friend was in good hands.

This was far; far from the truth, James was neither responsible nor dependable. This made it hard for Ivete to accept that she was being pushed out to make way for James. Ivete held true to her pledge, she always said that men come and go, but friends are supposed to be forever.

The more she thought about it the more she felt heartbroken knowing that Christina was throwing her life away. As more and more tears began to fall she sensed that the path Christina chose would be one full of pain, misery, and further abuse.

At times Ivete may be aggressive and at times, she may seem cold and heartless, but deep down inside there is a very sweet and loving girl.

It seemed that the thought of her losing her best friend was overpowered by the fact that Christina's life and future were in jeopardy by James' reckless lifestyle.

She thought, "Maybe if I just back off a little Chris will come to her senses and call me so we can work this out."

She knew that she could never fully accept that Chris and James were together. Then asked herself was it really worth losing the sisterly bond that Chris and she had? After all, if she completely walked away where would Chris go for salvation and refuge from the anxiety of James' antics?

"That girl needs me more now than ever, if I walk away like this, then I would not be a real friend, she needs my ass."

As these thoughts ran through her head, it was as if someone poured gasoline on that little flickering flame, which was almost extinguished by tears of sorrow, causing a massive explosion, and reigniting that Latino Fire everyone has grown to love as Ivete.

"Fuck it; she knows where to find my ass. As much as I don't want her to find out the truth about James, maybe this is exactly what she needed. I only hope when it happens she can bounce back, but you can bet all your money I'll be right there to stick my Nikes so far up his ass he will get chills every time someone says "Just Do It!"

Meanwhile, back in the house, James exits from the bathroom and walks toward Chris. "I thought I told your ass I didn't want that Dyke bitch in my house?"

"But I didn't she let herself in because you told me not to answer the door." She replied.

"I don't care she doesn't need to be here or all up in my business." he quickly adds. And, Chris promptly responds back to him, "This is not your house it's mine."

He swiftly jumped in her face, "See, just having Ivete around has you thinking you're brave."

She attempted to respond, but was silenced by a swift punch to the face. When her face met his fist, her knees buckled and she dropped to the floor. James followed up his first blow with a barrage of punches to her body and her face as he stood over her.

"James, please stop." In desperation, she called out.

Yet, he continued punching her until out of desperation she mustered up enough courage to swing back. She pushed him away with her legs giving her enough time to get to her feet.

They both stood facing each other exchanging blow after blow and for once, it appeared to be an even fight. Christina threw just as many punches, if not more as James and it was at that moment it dawned on her, why Ivete pushed so hard for her to take kickboxing. It was not to lose weight, but to teach her how to defend herself against James.

The many weeks of class consisted of tedious technique drills and many sore nights recuperating from them. She was starting to see how it was paying off and with big rewards.

James had no formal training hence his punches were wildly thrown and not connecting with the accuracy of Chris's kicks and punches. Hers were well timed and thrown with one sole purpose to connect with their target. It was a clash of technique versus power with technique having the dominance.

Chris had the upper hand, until James took her down, grabbing her legs at the hips and driving his shoulders into her midsection causing her to fall on her back. He then climbed on top of her and struck continuously until she was unconscious.

Several hours had passed before she came to. She got up cautiously thinking James was still around however, he ran out when she lost consciousness fearing that he had beaten her to death.

She went to her bathroom to evaluate her injuries. "Hmm, not bad a bloody nose, a small cut on my lip and a light bruise left cheek." She said as she looked in the mirror as blood dripped continuously, then she wondered what type of condition James was in, she thought "If this is all I have, then he's gotta be hurting."

However, hurting was an understatement, James was in excruciating pain from the numerous kicks Chris threw to his ribs. It felt as though someone had stuck a knife in between each rib, every gulp of air felt like someone was twisting and turning that knife.

She went to her linen closet to get a washcloth to clean the blood and smeared makeup from her face. Reaching for the doorknob, she felt a popping sensation in her right hand. When she looked at it, she saw that her knuckles were swollen and discolored. She then wrapped it with a towel and called China.

After the last confrontation over James, Ivete was that last person she wanted to call. She just could not deal with the many I told you so's that she would be forced to endure from Ivete's very opinionated mouth.

"Hey China its Chris, listen I need your help. Do you think you can take me to the hospital?"

China not knowing the series of events that took place that day replied, "Sure Chris, but what's wrong are you Okay?"

She thought carefully before answering not revealing too much that might tip China off to what really went down, "Yeah, I'm okay I just hurt my hand and it's swelling so I want to get it checked out that's all."

China now inquisitive, "You hurt your hand, how?" Chris quickly thought of a lie she could tell that would cure

China's curiosity. "I accidentally shut it in the door or something."

Hearing her response put China on full alert. She knew from the many other times that they had to take Chris to the hospital that the "or something" was mostly like associated with James.

Therefore, she questioned it a little further, "Wait a minute, you hurt your hand so bad for it to swell, but you don't know how you did it?"

"Ah yeah." Chris replied. But, China wasn't buying it. "Girl, do you think you're talking to Boo-Boo the Fool? Now tell me the truth this time what really happened to your hand?"

Chris paused for moment to think, "OK, I will tell you, but first you must promise me that you will not mention any word of this to Ivete."

This was totally out of the ordinary to keep something like this a secret. They all shared everything, so this made China ask more questions. "Why shouldn't I tell her she'd want to know if you're hurt? And why would you put me in a situation that would have me to betray her trust in me?"

Nervously Chris replied, "We had a fight concerning James." China instantly adds, "So what else is new, you two are always bump heads on the subject of James." Then Christina continues, "Well it's a little more to it than that, I kicked her out and told her not to come back until she accepts James."

Completely blown away by what she just heard, "Chris, how dare you put some man before your girl? You and her are like sisters and no one should come before that."

58

Unenthusiastically Chris replied, "I know, but she needs to respect that fact that James and I are in love."

China doubtfully questions, "In love? Is that what you really think?" Mystified by China's inquiry, "Yes, he loves me."

"Chris, who are you fooling? If James loves you, then why is he knocking boots with half of the tramps in D.C.?"

She remained silent as China continued, "You kicked to the curb, the only person in the world who loves you like family, over some unemployed mooching freeloader. Chris when it comes down to your girls or your man the choice is very, very clear men will come into your life and leave you in a heartbeat, but your girl will always be there for you."

This made Chris feel so small that, she did not say a word she just remained silent.

China then questioned her about what happened. "So you and James got physical?"

This matter made Chris even more uncomfortable for now she would have to admit for the first time that James was the lowest of the low. She had to reveal that he put his hands on her again; it didn't seem so embarrassing unlike the many times before whereas she felt a need to cover for him.

This time she was proud to tell what happened. This time she could say that she fought back and fought back well.

"After she and I had it out about him being there, then he came at me. A few words were exchanged and then he hit me." This angered China, "He's an asshole."

She commented as Chris continued, "So I hit him back and the next thing I knew we were going toe to toe and I was doing quite well until he tackled me. The last thing I remember was getting up off the floor with a bloody nose and my hand was hurting."

Upon hearing the news that Chris finally fought back China asked, "Is he still there now?"

Chris laughed, "No he ran off, he's probably nursing his pride and his ribs."

Puzzled China asked, "Nursing his ribs?"

Then with arrogance Chris proclaims, "Yeah, I hit him with at least seven good solid kicks to his ribs, so they should be real sore about now. He's lucky I didn't break them, I think my hand hurts from connecting with that big forehead of his over and over again."

This news brought a smile to China's face, "Good, he needed his punk ass kicked."

Then she changed things up a little. "You see these are the type of things that we share with Ivete."

Chris could not dispute this fact, but changed the subject to why she called China. "Girl, while you're over there playing 21 questions, my hand is getting bigger and bigger are you going to come get me or do I need to call a cab?"

China asked why do you need me to drive you?"

"Girl, you know my car has a stick and it would have been quite difficult for her to hold the wheel and shift gears with one impaired hand.

"OK, we're on our way." China said. Chris was a little puzzled, "What do you mean we, you're not coming by yourself?"

Nevertheless, China was not taking any chances, "Hell no, I'm bringing Nee just in case James comes back, I don't trust his ass." And, within a couple of minutes, they were on their way to the hospital.

The wait time before Chris saw a doctor was rather short. The doctor took a few x-rays and diagnosed her injury as just a sprain. It wasn't anything that an ace-wrap and some painkillers couldn't fix.

Chris exited from the examining room area, after receiving instructions on how to care for her injury. "Where's Nee?" she asked as she approached the waiting area.

China looked very disturbed, a look that made Chris questions her further, "What's wrong?"

China quickly got up and shuttled her to the door. "Come on let's go."

Chris still puzzled hesitated, "Wait where is Nee?" China didn't answer she just kept pushing her out the door.

Then it happened the one thing China was trying to avoid, they bumped into James.

"Nee, you were supposed to stall him." China lividly vented.

"I tried the best I could, but I don't like him as much as you do. So it's only so much we can talk about." Nee swiftly replied.

When Chris saw James, she froze in her tracks this time however, an unfamiliar feeling came over her. For once, she didn't have an ounce of thoughts towards him, nor even the slightest desire to speak.

But he sure did, "What the fuck you looking at?" He barked out as he looked over at her. She remained calm, channeling her thoughts to the look on his face when her first kick connected with his ribs.

She smiled then turned to China, "Let's go."

Nevertheless, James took offense to her cynical grin, "Oh, so you find it amusing that I'm here?" She didn't answer so he continued, "You're the reason why I'm here, Bitch."

His audacity made her then turn to say. "How does it feel James? Now, you know what I have gone through for the last few years."

He suddenly lunged at her but China stepped in his path. "No you don't." This made James irate as he raised his hand about to strike China, but Nee grab his arm and spun him around. "You're really fucking up now, Playa." Then pointed to China, "You see this is mine." He moved closer to be sure that James could hear him clearly, "If you have a problem with her then you to take it up with me, got it."

For a few moments, it appeared as if it didn't register with James, so Nee reiterated, this time he was more direct. "Raise your hand like that again to my Lady, and you will have a hell of a lot more than just a few sore ribs. Do you feel me?"

This echoed in James' head for a few seconds, and then he dropped his hand and walked off. Nee did one last thing to ensure that the episode with James was done and over. "I think you have something that belongs to Chris."

Puzzled James turned around as Nee stuck out his hand. "Give me her car keys."

This gave China goose bumps; she knew how much Nee loved her. Yet, the sight of him defending her honor her without hesitation was chivalrous and so appealing to her. "You see that Chris, that's the type of man you need in your life. In fact if I could clone Nee I would clone him just for you, because you deserve nothing less."

China statement spoke volumes to Chris she really started thinking that James didn't deserve to have a woman like her.

"Ya know China, you, and Ivete are so right, I do deserve better. I can do bad all by myself and I don't need James."

"I know that's right." China proclaimed as they all exited the hospital.

SALVATION

The stint of three months had come and gone so quickly it seemed to be a blur for everyone except Christina. To her it seemed like an eternity, she spent the majority of her time at Ivete's place and at times when she felt like being a third wheel, she would hang out with Nee and China.

Since James was no longer, there her house appeared to be barren and lifeless. Most would revel in the serenity of the peace that silence produces, but for her it was frightening to start over again.

Ivete remained vigilant in her quest to get Chris to see in her own words, "Men are an accessory and not a necessity."

She felt, while it was good to have a man in your life, he should not be acknowledged as a requirement. To give any man that much power meant surrendering all of your dignity and doing that with a poisonous man such as James was a road to self-destruction.

It proved to be a hard battle as she was met by much opposition; James' influence was still prevalent and played a very intricate role in everything that Chris did. It was always James this, and James that or James says this or James says that, until Ivete could not take it any longer.

"Look Chris, James is just like dashikis and doo-rags, played out. I don't give a flying fuck what he would do or say, So stop bringing his tired ass up."

This took Chris by surprise as she paused in shock as Ivete continued. "Girl, don't look at me like that, if his sorry ass was half the man he's supposed to be, then I wouldn't have that much of a problem with him."

Chris attempts to defend him, "Vette, you never liked him from day one. Why?"

Did she really have to ask why? Even more, she prepared herself for Ivete's answer. Nonetheless, she asked for it so Ivete gave it to her. "Chris, you can't be fucking serious."

Chris responds, "Well you don't know him well enough to know that he has a good heart."

"That's bullshit and you know it., Chris." Ivete said in disbelief. Then she adds, "I bet you that for every good thing you can say he has done for you, I can give five bad things he has done that would overshadow the good."

Chris then asked, "Why don't you give him a chance?" However, Ivete felt it was time to reveal something she had kept to herself until now.

"I tried, when I first met him, but the first time your back was turned, he squeezed my ass and the asked me for some. What kind of shit is that?"

Hearing this confession hit Chris like a 12 gauge shotgun blast to the chest. She had no reason, not to believe her. "Why am I just hearing of this now after four years?"

"Chris, I wanted to tell you, but I thought if I shut him down right, then and there it would not be a problem. Yet, I had no idea that he would continue to try this on everyone. Ivete said with a little compassion.

Remorsefully Chris asked; "Can we make a deal that we should never let a man come between us again?"

Ivete without haste answered, "Oh I can keep up my end of the bargain, but can you? Frowning up her face, "Because, last time your ass was straight up tripping."

Chris smiles, "Yes and it will never happen again.

"Ivete took a little more time to drive her point home, "OK Chris it really hurt to know that you put me second to him after all I have done for you. If it happens again, I will not be so forgiving."

Chris offers her a little more reassurance, "Oh no Girl, never again."

"That's good to know." Ivete adds. "Hey let's all go out tonight to celebrate your newly claimed 'single status'. However, as Chris began to speak, Ivete cut her off, "And I am not going to accept 'No' for an answer."

Chris a little uncertain replies, "All right, if it's like that." Ivete adds. "Oh, it's more than like that. You were going with us whether you agreed to or not, even if we had to kidnap your ass."

Chris was just as happy as Ivete to know that they were on good terms again. She also realized that Ivete was only acting in her best interests. As the time grew nearer, it became more obvious that a girl's night out was what she needed just girls like the old days.

It seemed like ages passed since the three of them had fun out on the town. Maybe a carefree night with no worries would do her some good. She had no idea; Ivete had a special treat in store for her. They all decided that would go out to Happy Hour later that evening at Mythology Nightclub.

China and Chris arrived at the club around 8:30pm they could hear the bass of the music as it seemed to be sucked out by a force of air each time the door was opened. The very clear and distinct sound of women cheering also reverberated from wall-to-wall and then back again. They joined Ivete just as she polished off her third drink and a few minutes later, they ate.

Yet, unknown to Chris, Ivete cunningly chose this particular club for one reason only. The one night of the year where the best exotic male dancers from around the country would all be in one location.

She was knew her old friend Mr. Anaconda would be there. He was someone she met several years ago at a Starbucks coffee house. She knew he could put a smile on any big girls face, because they always put a smile on his. He loved women of size and there was nothing better than to have some big thick thighs wrapped around him during his routine.

Mr. Anaconda was indebted to Ivete for the many favors she did for him in the past. She cosigned for him on his auto loan and she loaned him money to go to school. Therefore, he would be more than happy to accommodate any request she had.

What she was asking of him on the other hand was not a self-indulgent request it was more of a charitable gesture. She wanted him to do something that would help Chris realize that there are men out there that adore big girls.

Men that know, how to treat a lady and men that looked so tantalizing, succulent and not beat up or rundown like James.

As China and Chris sat down at the table joining Ivete, a little tipsy she yelled out "Damn, it took y'all long enough to get here." Chris responds "Hey Vette, what's good?"

China on the other hand being quick-witted fires back, "Oh girl stop bitchin and just have a good time. This is not about you or me it's all about showing Chris a good time."

This somewhat puts Ivete back in line as she then turned her attention away from

China and placed it on Chris. "Yeah, it's about celebrating Christina's break up with Mr. Dipshit and newly found freedom." Ivete says as she raises her glass in a toast.

China nudges Chris, "Looks like this heffa has been toasting all day, and we gotta catch up. What are you gonna have?"

Hesitantly Chris answers, "I don't know I have not been out since I got with James."

Just then, Ivete jumps in letting the alcohol speak for her, "Look, y'all fucking up my buzz. Let's set some ground rules up in this bitch right now."

She slurred and continued,

Number 1.

> This is 'Girl's Night Out', so there is no motherfucking Nee, Bruce and there sure ain't no sorry ass James.

Number 2.

> What happens here tonight stays up in this bitch.

Number 3.

> We came here to have a good time and we ain't leaving until this muthafucka shuts down.

And number 4.

> If I got some fine ass honey grinding his big black dick all up on me, keep your got damn hands to yourself."

She would have kept going if the waiter had not arrived to take China and Chris's order.

"Hello Ladies my name is Anton, I will be your waiter this evening. Can I get you anything?"

Ivete now even more belligerent pointing to China, "This one here, she's siddity she'll have a Merlot and get the other one well, she's a light weight. So, get her a Strawberry Daiquiri. As for me I'll have another one of these."

China inquisitively asks, "Ivete what's that?"

Ivete smiled then takes a sip; "I'm getting a *Hot Dick* now so I'll be just right when I get a real dick later." She then laughs.

China mumbles, "You nasty."

Ivete hears and responds, "Oh Trick, don't look at me like that, and I'm not nasty. I'm just a woman that knows what she wants and goes out to get it. Unlike those other Tramps out there, I don't do it for money, I do it cuz I want to."

China rolls her eyes around as Ivete continues, "I see, I want, I get, while other women sit around waiting for a man to approach them playing hard to get. If they say closed mouths don't get fed, then a pair of tightly closed legs doesn't get dick."

China mumbles again, to Chris, "This chick has really lost her mind."

As Ivete goes on, "The only difference between me and other women, is other women sit around playing this game waiting for a man to approach them, holding on to the pussy. Pussy is like water in a glass, if someone doesn't drink it, that shit will dry up. But, fuck all this talk; I came here to see some asses jiggling and some dick wiggling. So, get out my way."

She stands up and shouts, "Where is the dick at? I want some dick at my table."

A bit disgusted China comments, "See Chris, this is why I stopped going to clubs with her, she doesn't know how to act."

"Yeah she doesn't, but you gotta love her, she may be loud and rowdy, but she does keep it real." Christina adds as she looked over at her as Ivete grabs one of the dancer's love stick and began smacking her face with it. "Yep she keeps it real, slutty, but real."

As the night went on China and Chris began to loosen up a bit. Chris more than China, because China knew that too much alcohol around half-naked men was nothing but trouble for a woman that was about to be married.

Chris however, had no inhibition or hang-ups it had been a long time since she felt this type of liberation. She was like a kid in a toy store there were men of all shapes and sizes hungry for a dollar and she had plenty to give out for those who really wanted to work for it.

China took on the unofficial role of the mother hen the so-called designated driver and cock blocker. You know the one who would keep their senses enough to keep the other two from finding themselves in unbecoming positions.

All the men there were nice looking and all, but there was only one man that could cause her panties to become moist and make her kitty purr and that man was Nee. Therefore, she just watched her girls have a little fun, but Nee was in for it when she got home.

Then she noticed that Ivete had disappeared. She scanned all the dark corners of the room anticipating having to rush over and get her girl out of a compromising position.

To her surprise, China found Ivete at the bar having a conversation with Mr. Anaconda. She found this odd because he seemed to calm Ivete's rowdiness to where they were engaged in a civil conversation, so much it sparked China's curiosity so she walked over to assess the situation.

"Ivete, is everything okay?" China asked and Ivete responded, "Yeah Girl, I'm fine."

China then asked, "Who is this? Y'all appear to be a little close over here."

"Oh Mr. Anaconda, he and I go way back like four flats on a rusty Cadillac." She turned to introduce the two to each other, "Mr. Anaconda this is my girl China, China this is my old friend Anaconda."

China a little leery spoke, "Hi, nice to meet you."

And, he did the same, "Hi".

To ease her mind China tactfully inquired, "So how did you two meet?"

Mr. Anaconda began to speak, but Ivete answered the question before he could get out a word. "A few years ago, I was in a bad relationship with this guy who was abusive, I mean a real dickhead." This totally caught China by surprise for this was not the Ivete she knew. "What, not you?"

Ivete knew that this newly revealed information would spark nothing but questions from China who she sometimes referred to as Ms. CSI.

So to eliminate any possible cross-examining from China, she fully explained. She told her about the guy being a real jerk and he'd beat her on the regular basis. Then, one day, she said enough was enough and started packing up to leave him.

Then just when she thought she had gotten away, he came home caught her and a fight ensued. If it were not for Mr. Reliable, he would have beaten her to death. Therefore, with gun drawn on him she left. With no place to go, she drove around town for hours, until stopping to get a cup of coffee at Starbucks. That is where she literally bumped into Mr. Anaconda spilling coffee on both of them.

After apologies were exchanged, a conversation transpired that went up until closing time. It was just by chance that he made it known that his roommate/girlfriend had run off with someone else leaving him to carry the full load of paying the rent on his overpriced apartment.

Which was the reason he was there, he had just had a horrible interview with a prospective roommate and had little faith that he would find one as quickly as he needed.

Ivete saw this as more than a chance meeting, he needed someone to share a place with, to split the rent, and she needed a place to stay. She saw this as a blessing; bumping into each other was not by accident, but was an act of Divine Intervention. They were as true as true friends could be; it seemed that they were always there when the other got in a jam.

Ivete closes, "And from there a deal was set and I moved in within hours, now 10 years later here we are."

Although she heard the story, it was not the entire story; China was still caught up on Ivete being a victim of abuse. Then, all of the pieces of the puzzle began to fall into place as to why Ivete acts as she does.

Now there were answers to questions that she had about Ivete. There was clarity to as to why she was so hard, cold, and cruel towards men. It was a shocking revelation that was long overdue.

Yet, at the same time, it was also very touching and from that moment on, China never saw Ivete in the same light. She knew that for every cold and derogatory word that left Ivete's lips was one that was not filled with hatred yet, consumed with pain. China a bit relieved knowing that Ivete was in good hands with an old friend, switched her attention toward Chris.

Now with China gone, Ivete gets back to the task at hand. "Anyway, I think you will like Chris she's a sweet, kind, and caring person." His face lit up, "Okay, she sounds like a nice person"

Ivete was pleased, "Tell you what, why don't you give her a special dance first, like it's her birthday or something." she said with a crafty smile on her face. "Okay, that sounds like a plan, go back to your table and I'll meet you both there my set is next." He then left to get ready for his set.

Ivete rejoined Chris at the table and China soon thereafter, as the Master of Ceremony speaks, "And now, what you ladies have been waiting for—it's time for our featured dancer. All the way from up the street and around the corner, Washington D.C.'s finest. The one and the only, Mr. Anaconda."

The screams from the women was so loud, it seemed to repress the thunderous bass of the music to a faint whisper. Mr. Anaconda has always been a crowd favorite he adored all his fans just as much as they loved him. A self-proclaimed size-sexual, it didn't matter if she were fat or skinny, short or tall. He saw all his admirers the same and what they were beautiful women.

He would always spot one woman in the crowd that appeared to be somewhat different from the others. Someone who may, march to the beat of their own drum or a little bit reserved and shyer than the others, she was sure to get all of his attention.

He always wanted everyone to enjoy his performances, and but, it was the introvert wallflower that always piqued his interest.

Mr. Anaconda stepped out onto the stage, a six foot-four, 200 pounds of well-chiseled piece of Brown Butter Spice Cake, garnished in snakeskin chaps, with a matching snakeskin vest and G-string. On his face, he wore a black lace mask that matched his black moccasin boots.

The G-string fit his voluminous shaft into what was patterned to resemble the very snake of which shared his name. It was obvious that it took him some time to compress every massive inch of his package into it because it was tighter than a nun's cootie-cat.

The mere site of his exquisitely forged body had all the women mesmerized with every gyration of his hips. As he made his way from table to table earning a few dollars here and there, doing what he does best to make his money.

Nevertheless, he was on an assignment, a search and destroy mission. His primary objective was to find the table where Ivete and China sat, then single Chris out and do everything in his power to have her going home with panties that were soaked and dripping.

At the table, Ivete plays her part exceptionally well. "Oh Chris, girl look at his fine ass and he's coming this way too." Just as Chris turned around there, he was in her face. Busting with excitement, "Well got damn." Christina said, as all of his 8 ½ inches dangled before her just in hands reach, yet she was hesitant at first to make a move until Ivete gave her a little assurance.

"Go ahead go for it, remember what happens here stays here." So she summoned up enough courage and grabbed him...grabbed all of him.

In addition, Christina did just that, with her hand around his massive shaft her fingertips barely touched as she caressed him as though she had done it many times before. "Wow, he is three times the size of James." It was at that moment Ivete corrected her, "Look, I told you that I didn't want to hear shit about him, fuck his bitch ass."

She had never seen man of his size in person before although she had heard a bunch of stories and thought they were exaggerated. Yet, now she knew the many stories she heard all were true and wrapped up in a nice buff package.

"Look at her; she looks right at home with all that in her face." Ivete commented to China who was a bit turned off. "Damn, does he really need to be that up close and personal?"

"Oh it's all in fun, don't be so uptight." Ivete said as she moved behind Mr. Anaconda grabbing one of the complimentary towels from a nearby table and wrapping it around his waist.

She then started grinding on him as she slyly pulled his G-string to the side exposing the base of his pipe. This was what he and Ivete both agreed would be the signal for him to give Chris the special treatment.

Mr. Anaconda took full control of the towel tightly securing it around his waist then proceeded to remove his G-string taking Chris by complete surprise. Chris' heart began to thump as if it were going to rip out of her chest at the realization that just a thin piece of terry cloth separated her from his bountiful soldier of love.

He briefly pulled back to reach for a bottle of oil then returned and pour it all over his body. Chris quickly dropped her hands, but just as swiftly as they fell, they went right under his towel and around him.

He held her hand still allowing the motion of his body to massage the oil in. By this time Ivete saw that Chris was well on her way, but there was just one more thing that needed to be done although now was not the time. Mr. Anaconda continued to grind Chris's hands until she mimicked his motion.

She continued stroking until he backed off. He then pulled her up from her chair spinning her around; he placed one hand around her waist at belt level and the other on her back between her shoulder blades.

Then suddenly in one rapid motion, he bent her over in a standing doggy-style position, if it were not for the table being nearby to brace herself she would have somersaulted onto the floor.

He stepped back leaving her in that position, then unexpectedly just like Superman, in one single bound leaped up in the air landing on her wide voluptuous behind. Once settled he began humping on her furiously as if she was a bucking bull.

This made the crowd go so crazy, that their exalting approval was so ear piercing it diminished the thunderous reflexion from the DJ's sound system down to a faint whisper.

Mr. Anaconda did everything he could to make, this a night Chris would never forget. Ivete was also very pleased that Mr. Anaconda kept his word to show her girl a good time.

He spent a little more time with Chris then he moved on to the next table. However, he didn't fully extend his hospitality at the other tables as much as he did with Chris. She got the V.I.P. treatment that was only reserved for big tippers. Yet, he enjoyed her so much, he almost lost track as to why he was there to make money.

Chris took her seat back at the table, "Y'all that was so much fun and he is so, so sexy, thanks for bringing me out."

China smiled, "I'm glad you enjoyed yourself."

Ivete playfully added, "Damn, I thought you two needed to get a hotel room or something as much as you were all over each other."

Chris took another sip, "Oh, give me an hour and a locked hotel room with his fine ass any day of the week."

Coyly Ivete asks, "So do you want meet to him, I know him personally?"

"What can she really expect from a stripper, but a booty call?" China said appalled by her audacity.

Ivete not allowing that comment to go unanswered says, "Oh there you go again, China with your sanctified excessive mentality." China rolls her eyes as Ivete continues, "Not all of us are lucky to have a good man like Nee." China quickly responds, "I'm gonna ignore this and I suggest you do the same Chris, because she's crazy."

Ivete interrupts her, "Hey it's about being free and gettin yours."

China and Christina didn't say a word as Ivete continued, "It's like I said, all you women hold on to the pussy saving it for Mr. Right, but guess what? There is a time and a season for Mr. Right, but until that time why should I let this good pussy dry up?

She went on one of her infamous raves, "Fuck that shit, I'm gonna make sure my shit stays wet and in good working order whether it's with a real dick or a plastic one I'm gonna get mine."

She then turned to Chris, "Look Sweetie, you know I keeps it real right?" Chris nods as Ivete goes one "Pussy is the only commodity you can save that loses value over time. The older you get the more you save it the less valuable it becomes. "China agrees, "I know that's right."

Ivete persists, "You are in control of your destiny you can live your life with dick or without dick, but if you ask me? I choose dick when and how I want it then when he's done there is nothing for us to talk about I send him on his way."

She closed with a little humor, "And I always make sure that everything his ass came there with, he leaves with it. Don't leave your tooth brush, drawers, socks, watch or anything in my house because, no matter if it's two, three or four o'clock I will chase your car down the street to return his toothbrush."

Ivete's point was well received by Chris, but she quickly disregarded the possibilities of her and Mr. Anaconda getting together.

She thought, "This man has everything that a woman could want and can have his pick of any woman why would he want my big old ass?" And, it was on that note that all the girls decided to call it a night. So, they exited the club and drove home.

REVELATION

Six weeks passed and Chris had moved on with her life minus James. Although it was hard not have someone special in her life, thanks to her good friends she managed to get by.

James on the other hand, was miserable. When she kicked him out, he had nowhere to go, but back to his mother's house.

Ms. Jane gave him a place to stay, yet it came with strict rules, which he had to honor. The house rules he had to follow proved to be quite challenging.

She was a die-hard Christian who was virtuous and righteous so their extremely contradicting lifestyles always lead to a confrontation.

The rules she set for him were in her eyes not hard at all for the just. She took them directly from the Bible, the book of Colossians 3 verses 1 through 17....

1. *Keep your mind on things above, where Christ is seated at the right hand of God, not on worldly things.*

2. *Eliminate whatever is worldly in you: your sexual sin, perversion, passion, lust, and greed (which are the same thing as worshiping wealth).*

3. *Get rid of your anger, hot tempers, hatred, cursing, obscene language, and all similar sins will not be tolerated.*

4. *Do not lie.*

5. *Be sympathetic, kind, humble, gentle, and patient.*

6. *Forgive others as the Lord forgave you.*

7. *Everything you say or do should be done in the name of the Lord Jesus.*

8. *Giving thanks to God the Father through him.*

9. *Live your days with compassion, kindness, humility, gentleness and patience.*

And last, but most importantly

10. *Don't bring any weed or loose hoochies in my house.*

Sure, there were other rules, but they were not as important as the first seven. One was, if he was not in the house by 11:45pm he would be locked out.

She also said, "There is nothing open at midnight, but clubs and legs; of which both were the work of the Devil. She didn't want to invite Satan into her home so she double locked all her doors.

James felt these rules were too excessive for a grown 36-year-old-man to follow. It reminded him why he moved out in the first place. He wanted to live his life the way he wanted to and felt that he should set his own rules, but in her house it was either the Lord's way or you can't stay.

As much as he didn't like it, staying there was his last resort; and it seemed that not all the people to who he called friends were so friendly, when he asked if he could stay with them for a while.

Even the women he called his "jump-offs" didn't want to have anything to do with him.

Yet, they were sure to call like clockwork every month, when he got his unemployment check or he just bought some weed and when they called, he went running to them.

He knew more than ever that, leaving Chris was a big mistake, but his pride would not allow him to admit it to him or her. He also knew that Chris self-esteem was so low that it was just a matter of time before she'd be calling begging him to come back just like the last six times she threw him out.

He mapped out his plan, "I'll just chill at mom's place and when she calls, I'll rub her nose in it like a little dog and make her feel guilty about kicking me out then go back."

Contrary to his plan, Christina was having the time of her life. She did not have a dependent at home so; she had no reason to rush home.

Instead of rushing home by 5pm, she got home roughly around 11pm. Sometimes she didn't come home at all. She didn't realize until then, how much of her time was consumed catering to James' every wish. She always thought that going out to dinner or to a movie alone was depressing, but now she rejoiced in it.

She felt so rejuvenated; "Freedom, I never knew how much I missed you until now."

She could come and go as she pleased and do what she wanted when she wanted without hearing anyone complaining. Now with a clear mind and without the burden of having to be home in time to cook, she could spend a little more time with her clients.

This was something she thought would improve her sales. Devoting an extra hour or two, to sit down with customers to review all the properties viewed that week would be just enough to get them to decide on a house.

This fraction of effort would usually go a long way with those indecisive clients such as the Vanderbilts who were wishy-washy on everything whether it was agreeing on a house or anything else for that matter.

All it really took was just to remind them of the strong selling points of each property that both found to be appealing, then draw up a contract and it was a done deal.

Getting the Vanderbilt's to close on a house would be just the financial boost she needed. As their buying and selling agent, her commission on the sale of their 1.5 million dollar home would be nice.

However, her sales commission combined with what she would get when they purchased their new home would help get her caught up on all her bills as well as replenished her nearly diminished savings.

Mrs. Vanderbilt's knew she would make a pretty penny from them and it seemed as though she wanted Christina to earn every penny. It was nothing but the best as she was only interested in upgrading not downsizing.

After three days of persistently searching, it appeared as though she had found a house that Mr. Vanderbilt liked. All that remained was to convince Mrs. Vanderbilt that this was her new home. She was a tough cookie to crack, but Christina was determined to get her to bite.

She attacked Mrs. Vanderbilt alone and went for her weak spot, horticulture. Her vise was the cultivation of ornamental plants such as fruits, berries, and nuts trees.

"Mrs. Vanderbilt, I think we should take another look at the property on Market Street it already has a greenhouse and it would be prefect for your gardening."

The very meticulous Mrs. Vanderbilt corrected her, "No Dear, gardening is planting flowers, scrubs and pulling weeds. What I do is more extensive than that."

With her head held high with pride and distinction, "What I do is called horticulture, what some refer to as botany and it's a science not a hobby like gardening."

Christina responded with a little sympathy, "Oh I'm sorry I didn't know."

Mrs. Vanderbilt replied, "Oh, I'm not surprised it's not something that common folks like you would know anything about. It's more for those who are of higher and distinguished status."

Feeling insulted, Christina fired off a cutting comeback, "People of a higher status or just a fake ass ghetto chick that got intentionally pregnant by a ball player to get out the hood and thinks she's better than everyone else?" Christina looked her up and down is disgust," How did you do it? Did you lie about being on birth control or did you pick his used condoms out of the trash?"

Can you believe she said that to Mrs. Vanderbilt? Nah, she didn't, but that was what she was thinking. Yeah, that's right Zoe Vanderbilt was nothing more than an older version of Nee's ex Tiffany. A chicken head from the block that came up on some money and now thinks that everyone is below her.

If Mrs. Vanderbilt made that same callous comment a few months ago, it would be more damaging to Christina. Nevertheless, this was a new day and era; her attitude was not the same as it was when she was with James. Upon hearing Zoe's shrewd remark, all she could do was laugh.

In her mind, she thought of Mrs. Vanderbilt making that same statement to Ivete. She giggled even more as she almost could hear Ivete, "Bitch, I got your higher station right here, but it would be hard to get there with my foot stuck up your motherfucking ass."

It delighted her even more when she thought about China responding to the comment with her witty intellect, "Is that the same station where all you gold-digging skanks catch the bus?"

Zoe loudly snapped at her, "What do you find so funny?"

She turned to her and said, "I laughed because you made a comment about weed."

"So what about it?" Zoe nippily asks.

Suddenly without a second thought, Christina went on the attack, "Judging by the reefer burns on your lips and fingertip, I guess you would know a lot about weed wouldn't you?"

For the first time in her life, the outspoken Zoe Vanderbilt was at a loss for words. She could do nothing at that moment, but listen as Christina read her like a daycare storybook.

"I know the real reason why you have taken such an interest in the science of growing plants." She paused for a moment making sure that she had Zoe's undivided attention, then she continued, "It's because you're tired of buying somebody else's shit and want to grow your own weed don't you?"

Zoe immediately responded, "No, that's not true."

And, Christina retorted. "Come on, I know when someone is on the pipe."

Zoe fired back, "See you're wrong I don't smoke crack."

Christina failed to yield, "You are so right, you are too siddity to be on crack and by the looks of your burnt fingertips and black spots on your lips. I'd say you're more of a weed smoker."

At that moment, the almond colored skin of Zoe turned red as a baboon's ass. Christina didn't stop there, "I could smell the weed on you before you got out your car."

Zoe turned away in shame as she kept going, "Look, for the last two months I have been driving your ass all over the county showing you so many nice homes and each one you seemed to have a problem with."

Before continuing she shifted positions, "You need to stop wasting my time, this is the best house we've seen so far either you put a contract on it now or you turn it down find yourself another agent."

Christina took a step closer then whispered, "I don't normally get involved in other people's lives, but if I walk, your husband will mysteriously get an anonymous letter informing him about your little secret. So what's it going to be?"

Zoe paused for a moment then said "Don't just stand there let's get to your office and draw up the paperwork." All it took was a little persuasive reasoning and she would see it no other way.

Within a matter of days, she had the contract drawn up and ready for the Vanderbilt's signature. All she had to do was drop it off at their lawyer's office, the Law Offices of Hunter, Hines, and Jones.

She had never dealt with this firm before; she heard nothing but god things about them. It was late in the evening, but she did not what to hesitate. "I'll just run in real quick, introduce myself, shake his hand while handing him the contract, then I'm out."

The receptionist greeted her when she arrived at the law firm, "Good evening, and welcome to the Law Offices of Hunter, Hines, and Jones."

"Good evening to you," she responded back.

"How may assist you?"

She spoke as eloquently as the receptionist, "My name is Christina Jones and I'm here to meet with Mr. Hunter, I am the Vanderbilt's real estate agent and I have a contract for him to review on their behalf."

"Ms. Jones do you have an appointment?"

"No I don't, I spoke with Mrs. Vanderbilt yesterday, and she said that I could stop by at my leisure."

The receptionist spoke a little firmer, "I'm sorry Ms. Jones and Mr. Hunter have very busy schedules. If you don't have an appointment then you can't see him today." She then looked at his calendar, "The first available date that you can see him is on Thursday at noon."

"Ma'am, I really need him to take a few moments to review this contract so the Vanderbilts can move forward with the purchase of their new home."

"Well, the best I can do is to put it in his in-box." The receptionist said as she pointed to a mail-bin that appeared as though it had not been touched in a week.

Christina looked over at the overflowing bin, "No, I'm sorry I can't afford to do that. This is something he needs to review immediately."

Now with a little more sternness in her voice, "Miss, Mr. Hunter has a very demanding schedule you have two options: You can leave the document here by placing them in his in-box or you can mail them to him."

This somewhat upset her, there was no way she was going to let all the blood, sweat and tears she put into getting the Vanderbilt's to buy this home, go into a brim filled mailbox.

She insisted, "Look, I have to get these contracts signed by close of business today or else my clients will lose this property."

The receptionist stood up and reiterated, "If you do not have an appointment you cannot see Mr. Hunter."

It was at that moment a medium brown-skinned man a little over six feet tall approached them. "Maybe I can be of assistance." He was so broad he looked as though he could carry them both with one arm.

She took one look at him and it was as if the receptionist was talking as the teachers do in those Charlie Brown Holiday Specials. "Whaah–whaah–whaah–whaaah–whaaah–whaaah."

In her mind, she said, "Got damn, who is this sexy ass man?" Looking him up and down. "Look at your tasty ass, coming over here in that well-tailored pinstripe Steve Harvey Special offering to help and shit."

He turned then extended his hand out to her, "I work directly for Mr. Hunter perhaps I can help?"

The conversation continued in her head, "Yes, you can help; first you can look at me intensely with those big brown eyes of yours, then you can lick those delicious lips and get them all wet and shiny."

As they shook hands, she could tell that this man never had a labor job in his life; his hands were just as soft as hers were. Her hand seemed to disappear as his other large hand came around and concealed it.

"Why don't you step into my office so we can discuss this in detail?"

Still having not said a word to him she followed, yet if he could have gotten into her head, he would have heard. "Baby, I will follow your fine ass off the face of the earth, just lead the way."

"Sandra, I will take over from here thanks for your help." He said to the receptionist as he escorted her to his office.

Because she gave Christina such a hard time, Sandra received a dirty look as they went into his office. Christina found that she could not take her eyes off his tall wide frame.

As they entered his office, "Oh, I'm sorry I didn't catch your name." He said as he held her chair as she sat down. "My name is Christina, Christina Jones." "Is that Miss or Mrs. Jones.?" He appropriately asked and she quickly answered. "It's Miss. Jones"

"Hello Ms. Jones, my name is Maxwell Brown." He said in a soft and welcoming tone, all she could do was smile from ear-to-ear.

Her inner voice spoke to her again. "Damn Maxwell, I would love to do a little *'Sumthin-Sumthin'* with you *'Til the Cops Come Knockin.'*

However, she almost lost it when her inner voice said, "Yeah, as good as you look a sista could really develop some *'Bad Habits'* dealing with your sexy ass."

"Christina Jones?" He paused in thought, "You look familiar have you been her before?" Puzzled she answers, "No."

"It's just that I have seen you before and I can't put my finger on where." He said as he sat back in his chair.

"No, I don't think so, but I want to get straight to the point. I've already been here longer than I expected."

"So Ms. Jones what brings you into our office this evening?"

She let out a sigh of relief, "I have a contract for the Vanderbilt's that Mr. Hunter must review before they sign and it must be signed as soon as possible."

"And what type of contract is this?" inquisitively he asks.

"It's for the purchase of the property on Market Street."

"Oh, I recall a message I received this morning informing me that someone would be stopping by." He comments.

"Yes, I'm their real estate agent, so you should know why it is important that I get this signed immediately."

"Definitely without hesitation, I will be sure that this is the first document Mr. Hunter sees when he returns." He said as he grabbed a pen and paper. "Let me get your number and I will give you call as soon as it's complete."

She stood up opened her purse and said: "Here just take one of my business cards."

It was at moment, it came to him, and he knew exactly where I saw her before. He took the card as he escorted her to his office door. "Ms. Jones, I believe you and I have indeed met before."

She turned back with a puzzled look on her face, "Oh really where?" He didn't say a word as he continued to lead her to the door and then to the elevator.

By this time, curiosity had consumed Christina so, she had to ask, "We've met before, where?" She knew this had to be a case of mistaken identity; a sexy good-looking man such as Maxwell was someone who she couldn't forget.

He remained silent until she boarded the elevator and just as the doors started to close, he said; "Tell Ivete and China, Mr. Anaconda said hello."

Her mouth dropped open in disbelief as the doors close.

"Oh My God!"

IVETE & BRUCE

As the wedding grew closer, China's concern also grew. Never before, had she been put in a position where she had to choose between the two things, she loves the most her man and her mother.

"Nee, I can't believe you actually want me to choose."

He remained silent, gathering his thoughts before speaking, "I'm sorry China, but I just don't want that stuff in my wedding."

She quickly corrected him, "You mean our wedding, right?"

He recanted, "Of course that's what I meant, our wedding."

"Well, if it is truly our wedding, then my family should be allowed to participate in the ceremony."

"Yes, your family, but your mother's girlfriend is not really your family." He responded.

She corrected him, "Of course she is they're legally married now."

"No they are not," he snapped back with enough sternness in his voice reinforcing his belief. Then he continued, "Gay relationships are immoral and violate the traditional institution of marriage."

This was a similar argument that her father had when he first discovered that his ex-wife had left him for another woman, so she was prepared for it. Nee and her father were alike in so many ways that it seemed that they were almost the same person. Being that they were just alike China knew exactly where to attack to get him to see things another way. "Nee, so was Slavery." She shouted out leaving him bewildered.

"What? Woman, what are you talking about?" he asked.

She eagerly replied, "You want to talk about traditional institutions right?"

"Right." He answered not knowing where she was going with this.

"So, slavery was based on a traditional institution that went back to the very beginnings of time. Soon we realized the evils of that institution, and abolished it making it illegal. So that's what I think about the traditional institution."

With his main point shot down he said, "It's not normal and I for one don't like it."

"But Nee, in this day and age nothing is really considered normal." She paused in thought for a moment, and then cleverly said, "Most would say, that an average size man that finds a big voluptuous woman attractive is not normal. So that makes you just as abnormal as those who are in same sex relationship—right?"

In denial, "No, we're different we are not going against the grain of society."

She questioned this, "And why not, to the world I am not considered of normal size. So should I be treated any differently?"

He quickly answered, "No, you shouldn't, but—that's."

She interrupted, "No Nee, I know what you are about to say and it's not different."

"But—it's not" he tried to retort yet once again she cut him off.

"You're about to tell me that it's not the same and it may not be exactly, but the discrimination and the wickedness is."

He didn't say a word he just sat there listening as she continued, "Nee, you don't know what it's like to have people look at you like they're disgusted or make rude comments to and about you that you can hear clearly. Just cause you are not what they consider 'normal'. Do you?"

His once tight and inflexible body became relaxed, as he answered, "No, I don't."

"You have no idea how damaging it is." she added."

He didn't say a word as she moved closer wrapping her arms around him, "Baby, I don't want to argue about this any longer, please take some time to think about it."

The tighter her grip on him increased the more his body became less ridged and limper. "OK, I will."

"Come it's getting late let's get in bed." She said giving him a gentle kiss on the lips.

However, in her mind she was saying, "Yeah, let's go to bed so I can remind you of what you'll be losing if you don't agree to let my mother and Janice participates in our wedding."

Meanwhile, on the other side of town Ivete had just arrived home when she noticed a strange car parked in her driveway. Instantly, her survival instincts kicked into maximum overdrive.

She circled the block numerous times and with each pass, she studied the car making mental notes on every detail about it. The black and gold, BMW M6 Convertible, with a Georgia license plate and low profile racing tires with chrome spoke rims, but the one important factor about the car she could not detail. Who was inside? The tinted windows were so dark that she couldn't tell whether someone was inside.

On her sixth pass, she pulled over one block from her house, where she could maintain visual contact with it and had Mr. Reliable at the ready just inches from her hand.

"Who the fuck is that?" was a question that passed through her mind like a raging river.

She called her next-door neighbor Jennifer, to see if the car belonged to someone that was visiting. She knew that Jennifer would have asked if it were okay, the use her driveway before doing so, yet she wanted to assume.

Jennifer answered on the first ring, "Hey Girl, how ya doing, it's Ivete. Listen, do you have any guests at your house that may have parked in my driveway?"

She waited for an answer that would relieve her anxiety. Then her heart began to beat faster than a Russian racehorse. "Oh you don't?" she said as she glanced over at the car once more. "Oh really, you're out of town cuz your mother is sick?" Her breathing slightly increases, "Do you have someone house sitting for you?"

Again, she received an answer that, in no way could put her mind at ease, but if you were in the car with her, you would see no signs of concern on her face.

"No, nothing's wrong and don't worry I'll keep an eye on your house." she reassured Jennifer, but the twitching and clamminess of her hand told a different story. "Yeah, don't worry about things on this end I got it covered, you just take care of your moms and get her back on her feet— okay? I'll see you when you get back."

She tucked her cell phone in her front pocket, grabbed Mr. Reliable, pulled back on the upper-slide, and then letting it fly forward quickly locking a round in the chamber. She put Dr. Dre and Ice Cube's *Natural Born Killza'* compact disk in her CD player, letting the whining of the synthesizers with the slow, heavy beats further put her in a zone.

This was her favorite song so she sang along with conviction:

> *Journey with me into the mind of a maniac.*
> *Doomed to be a killer, since I came out the nut sack,*

*I'm in a murderous mind state, with a heart full of
terror.*

*I see the devil in the mirror. Buck-buck lights out!
Causes when I get my sawed off,*

Bitches get hauled off. Ha-ha!

Barrel one: Touches your motherfucking flesh.

Barrel 2: Shoots your fucking heart out your chest.

*You see I'm quick to let the hammer go click on my
Tec-9*

So if you try to reck mine.

Each verse that left her lips seemed to take her into a
deeper and darker place. She sucked down a big gulp of air
exited her car and began a stealthy trot to the strange car in
her drive way with Mr. Reliable in hand tucked close to her
right thigh.

She approached it from the rear creeping up the side,
she got close enough to peer inside, but to her surprise, it
empty. This discovery was unsettling which meant only
three things that could possibly exist. Someone stole a car
and dumped it in her driveway, another neighbor's guest
parked on her property or worse the occupants of the car
were in her house.

Still pumped up from the music she hoped for the
latter as she recited the lyric once more, "Causes when I get
my sawed off, Bitches get hauled off. Ha-ha! Barrel one:
Touches your motherfucking flesh. Barrel two: Shoots your
fucking heart out your chest."

She proceeded around to the front bumper of the car then over to her living room window where she knelt down to peek in. The mere site of a cigarette burning on the edge of her coffee table stifled any fear that may have been in her heart.

Yet, this was not just any ordinary table; it was her grandmother's table. This table was the only thing that did not burn in the fire that took her G'ma's life. To Ivete this table was the one and only thing that still connected her to her grandmother. She would sometimes talk to it just would talk to their loved one's tombstone at a gravesite. She treasured it as though it held her grandmother's spirit and to see a cigarette burning on it meant on thing, someone had hell to pay.

She pulled out the clip from Mr. Reliable checking to see how many rounds she could fire before she had to reload, and then shoved it back into place.

"Yeah, fifteen shots should be more than enough to drop whoever it is in my place."

She jumped to her feet rushed to the front door and burst in. She went from room to room clearing them, just as her father trained her and she passed on to Christina.

Back when she was little, opposed to staying at home doing normal things that the average teenager would do, talking on the phone or watching 90210, she would be performing repetitious drills repeatedly, only stopping when her father was satisfied. As much as she hated it, she never thought her acquired abilities would ever be called upon. Yet, somehow, he knew that a day would come she would have to call upon those very skills.

He always told her, when she would complain that she was tired. "I know that you think that is a waste of time, but it's far, far from it." He would say as he drove home. "Princess your mother and I can't always be there to protect you."

She naively replied, "That's what Davy, Paulie, Jake, and Joe are for."

He chuckled, "Princess, your brothers may not be around in your moment of crisis and there are times where things require immediate and extreme actions. You must be well-prepared at all times to neutralize those conflicts with extreme prejudice." He re-captured her attention as he continued, "What I am doing My Angel is teaching you what to do if you ever find yourself in a jam. But, more importantly, I am having you do this over and over again until you don't have to think about what to do next, you just do it."

Each room had obvious evidence someone was in her house. The living room had a lit cigarette burning on her grandmother's table that she quickly extinguished. The dining room table had a plate on it with a half-eaten sandwich and a used napkin. In the kitchen, all the ingredients that went into making the sandwich were still on the counter next to the refrigerator.

There were other traces that this someone was still there, in her bed there was a pair of black alligator shoes that appeared to be meticulously tucked away near her nightstand. This discovery made her even more furious.

Her grip on Mr. Reliable grew even tighter when she heard the shower come on. The continuous sound of rushing water magnetically pulled her closer to the bathroom door.

"Yeah motherfucker, I got your ass now." She whispered as she crept closer to the bathroom door. "You want to break into my shit, and then have the audacity to eat my food and wash your ass in my shower?"

Just as she reached for the doorknob, she was forced to alter her plan of attack because the water shuts off. Now there was a 50/50 chance that when she opened the door she may be face-to-face with an intruder that may also have a gun at the ready position ready to fire.

She could not help, but to think. "Did this person hear her and is now waiting to blast her as soon as she opened the door?"

Nevertheless, someone was in her sanctuary and must be dealt with and she was willing to go all out South-side Chicago style.

Just like the infamous Immortal Lords and Fallen Followers gangs from her old neighborhood, who would turn their peaceful block into a war zone riddled with gunfire.

China always asked her, "If you ever had to fire that thing at anyone could you?"

"I'd rather be judged by a 12 than carried by 6." Ivete would always answer.

That very philosophic statement was now putting her to the test and she was not going to fail. To her this was no time for a gut check; it was doing it to them before they do it to you. She took a step closer and with one swift motion twisted the doorknob kicking the door open.

The many hours of training that her father subjected her to, was now in full effect as she rapidly aimed Mr. Reliable at her target center mass. The barrel of her .40 caliber was within a few feet of the intruder and she had a good site picture of a tall brown silhouette of man with his back to her yet, looked so familiar.

His face could not be seen clearly it was cover by a dense layer of fog and the steam in the air was thicker than grandma's Sunday morning grits.

"Freeze motherfucker or you'll be leaving here in a body bag."

The outlined man did just that as he began to speak, "You wouldn't shoot a naked unarmed man in the back, would you?"

There was something very familiar about the sound of his voice, but she did not take any chances. She held the gun up still aiming dead center of the dark figure. A cool brisk breeze from the bedroom seemed to push away the murky cloud of stream leaving just the two of them standing there.

"Okay, now turn around real slow; I want you to stare at the person who is going to send you to meet your maker." She said wanting to see the face of the person that violated the sanctity of her home.

"Come on Baby, that's no way to welcome your man home now, is it?" He said as he slowly turned around.

Her mouth damn near hit the floor, "Bruce?"

"Yes, it's me."

"How in the hell, did you get in and when did you get back?"

He laughed, "Come on Darling, have you forgot what I do for a living?"

She lowered her gun and in a relaxed tone, "You could have at least warned me that you were coming into town."

"Warn you? You make it seem like you need to hide something from me."

"No, it's just that you could have called so I would know to expect you."

"And risk spoiling the priceless surprised look that you have on your face now."

"No, I would have been home to open the door instead of having you break in and scaring me to death."

"You scared?" He chuckled, "Now that's an oxymoron, looks like you were not scared enough to shoot me."

Like a bashful child, she quickly put the gun on a nearby dresser then shoves her hand into her back pockets.

"Oh I see you stepped up your game a little, the last time we were together you had that cute little .22, but now you have a Glock."

She tried her best not to smile, receiving his approval of her choice of firearm as he picked it up to look it over, "And I like how you've customized it nicely; hard chrome finish Raptor cut slide with TruGlo TFO night sights, KKM barrel, Falcon Grip system with Titanium 4 pound Trigger and a TLR2 laser light."

Her pride was getting the best of her, the more he admired her gun the harder it was for her to hold back her smile.

"It also has a skeletonized striker." She said bashfully rocking back and forth.

"Wow, you have really out done yourself, this is a work of art." He said truly flabbergasted by her well-crafted tool.

"And, I thought that you never paid any attention to me at the range, but now I see that you were listening."

He then reached toward the towel rack hanging behind the door removing his gun from its holster. His gun was a Nickel colored .50 caliber Desert Eagle that was a whopping 10 inches and weighed about 72 ounces.

It was so enormous, it dwarfed her six inch, 19 ounce Glock 27 making it look like a child's toy.

"Damn Bruce, that's not a gun it's a cannon."

He laughed, "Well, big men need to hold big things and not to jump off the topic, but have you been okay?"

"Yes why you ask?"

"You look smaller than I remember, are you sure you're okay?"

That comment unlike the first two was one to where she could not resist smiling. "Yeah, I've been doing a little kickboxing getting my Mixed Martial Arts on."

"That's good, but don't lose too much now, don't forget some of us, like women who are *fat-tractive* with a lot of fat-tributes."

"Oh yes Bruce, I know."

"Honey, you know that I will always think that you are sexy, but don't forget what Daddy likes." He said playfully.

"So if I became skinny you wouldn't want me anymore."

"Now you know that is not the case. I always dance with the girl I brought to the prom, but you know I'm kind of greedy when it comes to stuff like that."

"Oh really?"

"Yes really, you see all men like women with a nice sized breast, legs, hips and a lot of ass, but a man like me wants more than average. I want a four course meal and not a snack."

He gently grabbed her and embraced her tightly, "You feel me?" She seemed to melt like butter on hot cinnamon pancakes in his strong brawny arms.

Although he was not squeezing too tight it must have been the magic in the moment that seemed to force her to expel all the air out her body and not allow her lungs to be replenished them. There was just something about Bruce. He had some type of subduing dominance over her. An effect that was so commanding it turned the tough, unyielding roar of this lioness into a soft and cuddly purring kitten.

"Oh Okay, I won't lose too much." She said in a faint docile tone.

"That's my girl." He proclaimed in delight.

For a brief second, neither said a word holding each other as she placed her head against his bare rippled chest.

She let out a sigh, "I missed you so much and I hate when you have to leave like you did."

"And I missed you just as much, but you know that there some things in this world that we all must do.

Whether we like it or not there are just things that we must do, you know what I mean."

"Yes Baby, I know." She said with hesitation.

"Hey let's not talk about this now, how about going to dinner at our favorite restaurant." He asked.

"OK, but I would prefer skip dinner and go straight for dessert." She said as she pushed him on the bed and climbed on top straddling him.

It has been three years and 432 dead batteries since Bruce left, and now that he was home, she needed him bad. Her body was scorched when he held her body to his.

"Forget dinner, I want you close to me and on top of me, and I want you in me." She said insatiably.

He smiled, remembering how aroused he would get by her aggressiveness, so he let her have her way.

"I want you to make me drip all over you and I want to feel you inside me."

She leaned down to kiss him, which he greeted with the same in return. She ripped off her clothes throwing them on the floor. Fully nude on top of him, she slid back slightly to gaze at the imprint of his manhood as it began to swell from under the towel. Her mouth began to water and got just as wet as what she called her Dulce de Leche.

He grabbed her head gently, at the nap of her hair and pulled her lips down to meet his. The kiss reinforced what she believed deep in her heart since the first day they met. That no man could make her feel the way he did. It seemed that they were truly in harmony, he kissed the way she liked, and for her that was a good thing.

She had a few bad experiences, where someone tried to suck on her face, or open their mouth really wide and slobber all over her. Others appeared as though they didn't brush and had bad breath. Also, it would help if some knew the purpose of lip balm or petroleum, jelly, because to kiss a woman with cracked lips is not cool. The two types of kissers she hated the most were those that tried to suffocate her or those who rushed. She always said, "It's not a race to the finish line."

Yet, the way Bruce kissed was perfect he'd start with very gentle and slow pecks letting her lead and as it progressed, and then he'd then make his kisses more and more intense. It was so on point that her panties could have easily become soaked just from his kisses.

His kisses made her body go limp as a wet noodle, as her body collapsed on top of his. He hands wrapped firmly around her torso then slid down to her hips grabbing two heaping handfuls of her sumptuous booty massaging each cheek soothingly yet intensely. He knew her well, enough to know that rubbing her curvaceous heart shaped behind was the key to the Promised Land.

This seemed to elevate Ivete to the next level the more he kneaded her broad almond shaded cheeks the hotter she became. Then suddenly without interrupting their kiss, he rolled her over to her back.

Her buns still in the tight grasp of his huge hands, he slowly began to grind his fully erect member against her welcoming tightly closed curtains of love. Each grind and gyration of her hips helped the large mushroomed head of his pleasure pounder slowly teased apart her drenched labia.

She loved the way he slowly teased her, it always made her hotter than the hinges on the gates of Hell. She opened her legs wide to ensure the only resistance he would have was her swollen tight walls as his massive rigidness penetrated her inflamed honey patch.

"Oh Baby, please put it in." She begged as she broke from their kiss as her body began to shudder.

It seemed the more her sweet nectar poured out the harder he got. He was so hard it could have split a diamond in two and she needed it desperately. Her clitoris retracted under its foreskin so that it no longer received any direct stimulation. Her nipples became erect and the skin throughout her neck, breasts, and upper abdomen became dark, yet flush.

He didn't respond, he let his lips speak for him as they glided from her lips down to her chin, then he placed small pecks along her jawbone up to her ear where he mischievously whispered, "Do you really want it? Adding to her agonizing desire for him to be inside her.

Her answer was propelled from her mouth so quickly he could barely finish his question. "Yes Baby of course I do, now stop teasing me." She wept.

"If you want this dick, then you got to take it."

By this time, her blood pressure and respiration rate had doubled. Her heart rate increased from a normal 79 to between 110-175 beats per minute. It felt as though it was going to rip right out from her chest. Her body was on fire; her throat was dry wanting to be quenched by him.

"Do you love me?" He asked as he delivered stroke after stroke of his manhood.

"Yes, yes Baby I do." She roared from now tamed cynical thin lips.

He quickly found the right cadence as her body began to impetuously thrust back compelling him to vigorously go deeper and deeper. He continued until her thighs became tense, her back arched and her nostrils began to flare.

Just then, an intense recurring convulsion began to radiate from her love box down to her holy hole. The pulsating was mildly subtle at first then slowly intensified until it progressed into a heavy throbbing. The throbbing sensation traveled from her head through her spine and down to her genital area. She was on the edge of passing out as heated waves of energy appeared as though it were crawling all over her skin from the inside.

A hot sensation shot down her legs then spread all over her body. It gave her the strong, but familiar sensation that she had to urinate.

"Oh shit I'm cumming," thundered deafeningly from her lips in a long drawn out stutter.

Her body became stiff and firm then trembled violently. She raised her hips up off the bed as honeyed sauce splattered out covering both of them, at the same time her bronzed pearl, honey bun and even the treasured hole between her cheeks began to pulsate and constrict.

It was roughly twenty seconds later when these tremors diminished down to slight tingles. Bruce was so attentive to her in this euphoric state by holding her tightly through her complete passage to the other side. Slowly regaining composure, she unexpectedly rolled out from under him securing a mounted position on top pinning him down. His face ignited in astonishment, never before has she displayed this type of aggression. It took a lot of nerve for her to make an audaciousness move such as this and he knew it.

It was contradictory of the woman to whom he has come to know, yet at the same time enormously arousing. The mere fact that she has the heart to take this form of domination over him was just as intoxicating as a bottle of Patron Platinum.

She forcefully and aggressively clawed his rock-hard burly chest unrelentingly as she pulled her legs in closer to his body. The last of her tremors gone, she slid down between his legs to become face-to-face with his immensely blessed piece of virility.

It was the most beautiful things she ever saw, she could do nothing but gaze at it in amazement.

"He chuckled again then asked, "So now that you've got a firm hold of it; what are you going to do with it?"

"This?" She asked cunningly looking up at him while lightly pecking on the head of his swollen love muscle. Each peck was followed by a long and twisting stroke by both hands down his elongated throbber.

"Oh shit that feels good," he wailed as he started to twitch.

Every precisely placed kiss made him quiver, but he nearly jumped off the bed when his head finally made it past her lips and into her warm moist mouth. She took him in, stopping just at the base of the crown while simultaneously turning her hands and head in opposing directions letting her lips rain down enough to keep his shaft lubricated.

"Oh shit." tore from his lips four octaves higher than its normal tone.

Yet she kept working his mighty stick causing it to grow bigger and thicker with each beat of his now racing heart. She picked up her tempo moving so fast that the friction of her hands blended with his initial love secretions and the sogginess from her mouth produced a light lather that bubbled around his lustful package.

The sensation it gave him caused him to have no command over his body. Ivete had one more trick up her sleeve. It was a big gamble that he would or would not be receptive of it, but she believed she had nothing to lose if he wasn't down for it. She didn't care if things came to an abrupt end, she got hers in, and it was the biggest eruption she had in a long time. In fact, it was *orgasim-tastic*.

The mere fact that he brought her to a state of grace, so quickly and with little effort was something that would surely be the hot topic at the next Ladies Night Event. She cleverly without breaking stride, slipped her right index finger into his forbidden backdoor then gently massaged his prostate.

Within moments, he screamed out, "Oh Damn baby, that's the shit right there." encouraging her to continue until, "Oh fuck, oh shit!"

When he started to climax, she swiftly withdrew him from her mouth and aimed his passion pistol back up towards his chest. When he released it so massive it had such a force, it shot passed his chest hitting him on his chin. He eyes rolled back in his head and his body locked up becoming as inflexible as a board. He struggled to speak yet nothing but gibberish came out. The circuits between his body and brain, which regulated his motor skills, seemed to be impeded by each enormous palpitation.

She smiled to keep from laughing as the words he attempted to speak came out in a high-pitched squeaky voice that resembled that of a girl.

Although in a few quick squirts, it was over and to her disappointment, he rolled over to take a nap.

This did not go over well with Ivete, "Just like a fucking man." She said to herself as she went into her bathroom to take a shower. Ten minutes later, she exited the shower and Bruce had pulled one of his infamous disappearing acts.

RESURRECTION

After her little encounter with Mr. Anaconda, Chris quickly called China from her car. She tried to call Ivete, but there was no answer.

"Girl, guess who I just ran into?"

"I hope it was not that punk ass ex of yours." Still bitter answered with sarcasm.

Chris quickly corrected her, "No, I saw that guy that gave me a lap dance at the club the other night."

"You mean the one in the snake costume?"

"Yeah him, that's the one."

"Damn, where did you see him?" China inquisitively asked.

"I had to take some documents to the lawyer office of a client and this wench receptionist gave me a hard time. I was just about to let her have it, when out of nowhere he appeared."

"Really?"

"Yeah Girl, and he looked just as sexy in a business suit as he did in snakeskin."

"That good huh was he a lawyer?"

"No, he's a Law Clerk and I could not take my eyes off him."

"No, get out of here." China responded.

"It was like his body was saying more than his mouth wasn't."

"Really? What did it say?"

"It said, 'You want this shit, don't you?' she mimicked in a soft, but deep whisper.

"Wow." China said in admiration, "What else happened?"

"Tell you what, meet me at your shop in 10 minutes and I will tell you all about it."

Within seven minutes China was at the shop eager to obtain the details, this was something that was too juicy to pass up. Chris intentionally arrived a little later than planned. She knew that if curiosity killed the cat, then China would be dead and buried by the time she arrived.

She joined China at the table, paused for a moment before speaking, "Hey Girl, how you doing?"

"Look, don't play games with me." China uttered bothered by her weak attempt to stall. "You know damn well, I am not here for any small talk."

"Whatever do you mean?" Chris said in a condescending tone.

"You see that's how folks get that ass beat around here; so stop playing."

Chris adjusted herself in her chair then continued her story where she left off. "I had to drop of a few document for the Vanderbilt's at their lawyers office and." She purposely changes the subject, "Oh did I tell you that I finally got the Vanderbilt's to close on that house on Market Street?"

By this time China was a little pissed but in a lighthearted manner said, "Keep toying with me and I'm gonna stick my foot up your ass."

Finally having her fun, but even more getting the message that playtime is over she tells about how she ran into Mr. Anaconda.

"Yeah, like I was trying to say, this *bougie hoodrat* receptionist at the law firm acted like she didn't want to help me. No matter what I said or did, that Heffa just didn't want to assist me. I was just about to bust her ass when this fine ass honey came out his office."

China begins to smile in spite of all the B/S that Chris tried to feed her. She was somewhat pleased that she was getting to the interesting part as Chris resumed.

"Out stepped this gorgeous, six foot tall, medium brown skinned, 200 pound ripped piece of man candy."

"Get out of here, he look that good?"

"Of Couse he did why wouldn't he."

"Girl, you can't be too sure and besides he had on a mask so there was no telling what was under there."

"Who not him!" That man looked just as delicious as he smelled."

"Do you kiss your mother with that foul mouth?"

"Huh?"

"You've been hanging around that Ivete too long, now you're starting to sound just like her. Soon, you both will be running around here cursing like two Texas truck drivers and what's really bad is that it's starting to rub off on me."

"With your dirty mouth? Child please, you don't need our help you were doing well on your own."

Chris continues with her story, "Anyway, he led me to his office."

China interrupts, "Well, what is his name, did you call him Mr. Anaconda, Mr. Anaconda, Snake or what?"

"Look, are you gonna let me tell the story or are you?"

"I have to asked questions like this cause your ass be leaving out all the important details and shit, but go ahead." China commented.

"He told me his name, guess what it is?"

China didn't like this, "See this is what I'm talking about you wanna play guessing games, just tell me what his name is."

"His name is Maxwell." His name left her lips in a soft and smooth hue that made it sound majestic.

China repeated it just as she did, "Maxwell."

The way she said it, did not sit well with Chris, "Wait a minute ho, you already got a man."

Perplexed China asked, "What do you mean?"

"I thought you were so into Nee?"

China quickly answered, "Of course I am."

Nah I hear it your voice."

"What I just said his name, that's all."

"But it's the way you said it, that has me questioning you."

"Are you gonna finish or what I don't have all day." China said to take the attention off her apparent interest in Maxwell.

"Ok-ok-ok, I'll tell you the rest damn don't have a cow."

"Look forget all the details you're wasting valuable time. I just want to know two things. How do you know it was him that we saw in the club and did you get his number?"

"He told me at the elevators just before the doors closed and no, I didn't get his number."

"What? You're playing again, right?"

"No, I'm not playing, I didn't."

China was shocked to hear this, "Girl, you got another chance to see that fine ass man and you didn't close the deal?"

"Ah no." Chris answered.

"You had a second chance and you blew it, you dropped the ball. Man, your game is weak as shit." China proclaimed

"I guess?"

"Damn, I thought that you would at least be able to tell me that you are going to see him again."

"Wait, I didn't tell you that I wasn't going to see him again, because I will."

"What?"

"I have to go back to pick up the contract I dropped off."

China's whole demeanor changed instantly for there was still salvation, "Really? So when will you go back?"

"I can go back any time I want."

"Then, what are you waiting on?"

It was a long dead silence before China asked her question again, "Chris, what are you waiting on?" Christina still didn't say a word.

"Hel-looo?"

"Yes, I heard you."

"Then, tell me what's the hold up? Girl, you better go scoop up that fine piece of brown sugar before someone else does."

"Like who?"

China chuckled, "Like that receptionist that gave you a hard time. She probably wanted you gone so she could have him all to herself."

"You think so?" Chris asked with a pitiful sound to her voice.

"Chris, let me ask you a question?"

"OK what?"

"When you walked in who else was in the office besides Maxwell and the receptionist?"

"No one."

"And what time was it when you got there?"

119

Chris pondered for a moment the answered, "Around 8 PM."

"Eight Chris, 8 o'clock at night?" China doubtfully asked. "He may be a workaholic as most folks are in his line of work, but if the office is closed. Why was the receptionist still there?" She paused for a few moments before going on, "There is no real reason for her to be there, unless she has an ulterior motive."

Truly baffled Chris asked, "Yeah why was she there? Ivete's my receptionist and when I close my office for the day, she rolls over the phones to the answering service and runs out faster than diarrhea."

China fills her in, "She's still there because she is plotting."

"Huh, what do you mean plotting?"

"Chris think, if you wanted to get close to a coworker when is the best time to do it?"

"Well, I would go out for drinks."

"That's how they do it in the corporate world; let me school you to how a *Skeezer* does it."

Chris thought this was nonsense yet she entertained China's foolish idea anyway, "Okay, show me the *Skeezer* way."

"Oh, so you thinking I'm bullshitting you, huh?" she said as this squinted as China's skepticism. "Let me run down same game to you. She finds out when he is going to work late and then she finds a lame reason to stay late. She'll do this for about a week to a week in a half.

For the first few weeks, she actually works, but the other half, she sits at her computer either playing Solitaire or shopping online. She'll go all out, putting a small number of documents on her desk to make it look like she was actually working. She plays her part until she sees him packing up to leave."

Chris is slowly starting to find validity in all China is saying and wants to hear more and more is what China gives her.

"By this time he calls it a day he is tired and just wants to get as far from his work as possible, so he is not thinking clearly. She times it so, just as he walks pass her desk; she starts packing up and says 'Oh, you're leaving too? If he is talkative, that's the green light to proceed with step two of her scheme. But, if he is quiet she will put it off until next time."

China continues, "If, he has conversation then he is ready. She will have some sob story concocted either that her ride is late or her car is broken. This is part of her plan, it also a test to see if he is a decent guy and not leave her stranded. She is trusting that he will offer her a ride home."

It seemed the more China broke it down for her, the more she started to believe her. "So every time he stays late she will stay late, slowly easing her foot in the door or should I say easing her hand in his pants."

"Is it that easy?" China asks.

"Girl please, men are just like women we both are basically the same. Just like we get all gitty when a man compliments us on our beauty, they get goofy when you praise them for being so strong."

"Come on we all don't act like that." Chris declares.

"Yeah right, but that's neither here or there. What it all comes down to is that she is sitting back waiting for the one time where he gives her the right signal to go in for the kill. One ride home will lead to four and five rides home then to several dinners then one day when he drops her off, she'll invite him in. Once he crosses the threshold of her front door, he is doomed. Many men enter and they are never the same."

"How so?" Chris asks.

"If her game is really tight, she'll sit him down on her sofa with a bottle of Merlot and two glasses. She'll sit with him drinking it, but what he doesn't notice is that her glass will have two to three ice cubes in it."

"So, why is that a problem?"

"Chris, you are so naive."

"Why do you say that?"

"You see this is proof that you've been around that Ivete too long, because the only drinks she knows is brown liquor. For the record Ivete Jr., you are supposed to serve red wine at room temperature and not with ice."

"Oh so, she would be just as ghetto as me." China naively assumed.

"Nope, you're wrong again. She doesn't serve him wine with ice, silly. She puts ice in wine so it melts; therefore watering it down so it's not as strong as the glass he drinks. She does this so he will get twisted way before she does."

"Oh, I see now."

"Right, so then more he drinks the easier it will be for her to sink her claws into him. After that it's over, he will never be the same again because she'll excuse herself to change into something more comfortable. Yet, what she calls getting comfortable is having on barely any-thong on at all."

"Any-thong, you mean anything right?"

"Nope, you heard me right; I said any-thong, as in thong underwear. She is going to come out in something see through and sleazy with the full intent to seduce him."

"Get out of here."

"Yep, you can put that on everything. So now you see why you should not sleep on this?"

"Wow I had no idea."

"So, now you know, and what you need to do. Go back to his office to do what you do best, close that deal."

"Yeah, let me get my things and head up there right now."

"Wait, Chris you're not going to go up there dressed like this, are you?"

"What's wrong with how I'm dressed?"

China looked her up and down and said; "Well, it's Okay if you are going to meet him at the laundry-mat."

"Huh?" Chris inquisitively asked.

"Going after a man is just like fishing."

"What?"

"You heard me, going after a man is just like fishing. You have to use the right bait at the right time with the right presentation."

"Okay and you say this because?"

"Come; let's get you in the right attire." She took her by the hand and led her to the door.

After a short drive, they arrived at Chris's house. "Now, let's see what baits you have in your closet that will catch his eye." She went through Chris's closet with extreme scrutiny flipping through item after item, "Nope-nope-nope, no, this won't do. Pausing to look at one outfit then turning up her nose, "Oh hell no! Damn Chris, do you have anything that looks sexy and sassy and not home and garden in here?"

Chris didn't respond feeling somewhat offended by China's callous critique of her wardrobe. "Chris, you need an extreme, extreme makeover. There's no way you gonna catch a man with this shit."

"It's not that bad, is it?"

"It's okay if you like the Trampy Christian or the 'Hi, welcome to Home Depot. May I help you' look."

"That bad huh?"

"No, worst. Um let's go see what I have in my closet."

They drove clear across town to China's place and when they got there, Nee was sitting in the living room.

"Hello ladies." He said, noticing the look on China's face. "Oh, I know that look. You're on a mission, let me get my love and get out your way." He said, as he approached for a kiss, and then quickly backed away. "I was just on my way to meet Tony; he has something wrong with his car and wants me to take a look at it."

"Okay, did you want to go out for something to eat later?" She nonchalantly asked leading Christina to her closet.

"Sure what do you have a taste for?"

Muffled by the many walls that separated them "Italian would be nice."

"Cool, see you then." He said as he closed the door on his way out.

China then opened the door to her closet and they both walked in. Chris's eyes lit up, "Damn, is this a closet or a room?"

China laughed, "Oh that's right, you have not been here since we remodeled. Well, it's 9x9 feet this used to be our den, but we ran out of space in the bed room closet so we converted this room into a closet."

Chris gazed with awe into the closet. The left wall had a two tiered clothes racks that ran along the wall. At the rear wall were many shoeboxes meticulously stacked from the floor to about six feet in alphabetical order by hue.

On the right wall, there was a huge 69x52 inch traditional cherry wood makeup vanity table set with mirror. On the back of the door was a full-length mirror that covered the entire door.

"Damn girl, this vanity is bigger than the desk in my office at work."

"Yeah, it just a little something I picked up at a yard sale."

"And from the looks of things you may need a bigger room." Chris said and she browsed through China's wardrobe. "With all these clothes I see why Nee let you have this room as a closet there is no room for his stuff."

"Child please, when I first moved in I had only five pair of shoes, ten dresses and ten pair of jeans."

"Okay and?"

"That man had three times as many clothes as I did, so I had no choice, but to find someplace else to keep mine. So I moved in here and it grew to this over time."

"Get out of here." Chris exclaimed he has that many clothes?"

"Girl, he has so many suits that he now takes up not one, but two of our closets, but enough about that we are here to pick out something for you to wear that will surely capture Mr. Maxwell's attention."

China fished through her wardrobe searching for the right outfit that would even make Nee say 'Got-damn.' "Okay, let's see what you can wear."

She pulled out a crimson colored dress that had and on or off-shoulder neckline, draped surplice bodice, an Empire waist with 3/4 length sleeves and just-below-the-knee it flared out.

Next, she reached for a black knit dress with vertical ruffle front, elbow length sleeves, a flattering V-neck, stitched waist with bust darts for an enhanced fit. She laid everything out on her.

"Nope that's not it, not the look you want." So, she went back to her closet and repeated the process. This time she wanted to mix things up a little so she reached for a faux metallic leather jacket that had a mock neckline, and tabs at the hem. A shimmering foil accented and mixed animal print tank top and a pair of simple Ponte trousers that had a hint of stretch and a slightly slim-cut leg, and paired well with tunic-length top. Although, once she viewed these items together on the bed, they didn't appear to be the right look.

For a touch of class, she pulled out a basic white shirt that had a button-front placket that fastens to a regular collar accented with a black belt to enhance her figure by creating a flattering, subtly shaped silhouette. To go with the white shirt she selected a pair of basic five-pocket designer jeans crafted with a slender cut through the hip and thigh, to sit comfortably just below the natural waist. She felt that this was close, but it was not quite it.

Lastly, for sophistication she chose a black pencil skirt with an inverted front pleat split in the front and back with a satin red buttoned down dress shirt. Feeling that she was close she looked through her countless rows of shoeboxes stacked on the rear wall. She picked a box, inside was a pair of burnt red pumps unworn.

Just as many other women, they were purchased with no particular purpose in mind, but just because they were marked down for less than half of the original price. She didn't know if she would need them, but it was nice to know that they were there if she did.

To complete the ensemble, she added her Tiffany & Company Signature Pearl Necklace she got from her father as a gift on her sixteenth birthday. She added the pearls to the other items that were laid out on the bed.

"That's the look right there." She declared proud of her selection.

Doubtfully Chris asked, "Are you sure he is going to like it?"

China gave Chris a cold hard look, "If this doesn't turn his head, you need to move on cuz that means one thing."

"What's that?"

"He's gay."

"What?"

"If this doesn't get him to at least look at you, he must be gay."

"Wait, so what you are saying is if he doesn't look or stare that makes him gay?"

"Exactly."

"What if he's married?"

"If he is married, then he's just married, but he's not blind."

"What?"

"Married or not, there is no harm in noticing someone who is attractive. Nee and I are always looking at other folks that we find attractive."

"But isn't that wrong?"

"No, it's not wrong if there is trust and respect."

"So, you don't think it's disrespectful for Nee to look at other women around you?"

"No, not at all."

"I knew it was something wrong with you and now I know what it is, you're crazy."

"Crazy or confidential that my game it tight?"

"What?"

"I'm going to get straight to the point, what separates me from other women, really comes down to one thing."

"And what's that?"

"There is nothing I won't do for my man."

"Yeah, you and every other woman on the planet, so tell me what special about that?"

"No Sweetie, when I say anything I mean everything. There is no reason for him to wander to another woman to do something I should be doing. As his woman I am supposed to be his every fantasy as he is mine."

"I don't get it."

"That's right, you and many other women other. You don't get it, because you won't do it."

"Do what?" Chris asked a bit confused.

"Whatever he wants, if Nee wants to see a stripper, I'll be his stripper. If he wants a raunchy ho, I'll be that too."

"And do you, you know." Chris inquired as she pointed to her bottom and made a back and forth motion.

"Oh, do you mean do I take it in the booty?" China spoke so freely although Chris appeared to be a little bit uncomfortable with China's candidness about this subject.

"Uh yeah that's what I meant."

China did not hesitate, "No, I don't, but if Nee wants to do it, then I will try. But before we do, we must fully discuss it."

"Damn, that's crazy."

"Is it really crazy because I am willing to do anything to keep my man happy and most of all at home?" China fired back a bit offended by Chris's 'crazy' statement, "Look, the bottom-line is that if you please your man completely in and out the bedroom there is nothing or no one that can cause him to stray. So he can look all he wants, but he knows that no one can come close to what he has at home."

"Wow, you really believe that shit don't you?" Chris suspiciously questioned.

This struck a nerve with China so she rapidly fired back with, "Huh, if he is stepping out on me at least he's covering his tracks and not doing it in front of my face like other people I know."

"Ouch." Chris responded and China justified her insensitive response by saying, "Well, you went there first, but that is not why we are here. We are supposed to be getting you ready, so that you can start a new page in your life, a new page with Mr. Anaconda."

"True."

"OK, why don't you jump in the shower while I steam the wrinkles out the clothes?"

Fifteen minutes later Chris exited out the bathroom, "Here put these on." She threw a pair of black boy shorts on the bed in Chris's direction.

Shocked Chris replied, "I'm not going to put on your used underwear."

"Come-on now Chris, do you think I'm that trifling to give you my used underwear? If you look closely Ho you would see that the tag is still attached so they have not been worn yet."

"Okay, but what's wrong with what I had on?"

"No you've had them on all day so, they are not fresh also these have a soft, microfiber liner that has hidden hi-waist tummy control panels. They will make all your curves sleek and smooth in this skirt."

"If that's going to make all this this sleek and smooth then I want a box of them. She said jokingly as she put them on."

China closed by saying, "Look, we're going for a sexy look and those grandma bloomers you got on are not sexy at all."

As she put on the pencil skirt, "Ooh, with these boy shorts on this skirt just glides right up on my hips."

"Yeah, you need to get some for yourself it puts all your pieces in the right places and the control waist makes your tummy look trimmer and your hips and booty extremely curvy."

Chris viewed herself in the nearby full length mirror as she put on the shirt and the shoes, she was really getting into it. The outfit seemed to transform a clean-cut good-girl into a captivating *Diva-fied Enchantress.*

It altered her whole demeanor; her once repressed sex appeal seemed to erupt from a tightly sealed bottle and a once stifled confident spirit began to flourish. As her old clothing were removed and the new clothing donned it was just like the metamorphosis of a pupa changing into a beautiful Peacock Butterfly.

The change was so mystifying, that even China who put it all together questioned if this was really Christina standing before her.

"Damn Chris, that outfit looks like it was made just for you."

"You really think so?" Chris asked as she sashayed from one end of the room to another.

"Yes, but now you need to do something with that hair."

"What's wrong with my hair?"

"Ah, I don't think your frizzy ponytail works with the outfit, it looks kinda high school-ish. Why don't you ever let you hair down?"

"I like a ponytail cuz it practical and easy to manage."

"That may be so, but it's not a good look, no not at all."

China walked over to her from behind to remove the Scrunci that imprisoned her hair from freely flowing.

Once removed her hair it gingerly descended upon and covered the collar of her shirt. Christina's rich black hair had an off centered part and bluntly cut just below her shoulders. The bangs were chopped with a semi-circle covering her eyebrows.

"Now that is much better." China said as she peered over Chris's shoulder into the mirror verifying that Chris saw the same portrait of loveliness that she did.

Chris was engrossed in the sentimentality of the moment; for once in her life, she didn't need anyone to convince her that she was beautiful. No not this time, she saw that she was just as sexy and sensuous as the clothing she he was wearing.

A tear began to form in the corner of her eye, "I really am, pretty."

"Sweetheart, we all told you this, but you never wanted to believe us, but now you see what we've seen for many years."

"Yes, I see." Christina said with a sniffle.

"Okay, so now get all them tears out now because when I put on this make-up your little punk as can't be crying it will start to run."

Chris wiped away her tears then followed China over to her enormous vanity. "First we need to cleanse your face then apply a decent oil-free moisturizer." After that, she pressed a piece of facial tissue all over Chris's face to lift away excess moisturizer.

"Just so you know, you don't need to put on a lot of makeup, in fact no one needs a lot of make-up unless they are trying to hide or cover up something like the dark circles under the eyes after a night of little sleep."

"Really?"

"Yeah, the sole purpose of make-up is to highlight and accentuate the features on your face but in most cases it is not really necessary."

"Wow, I didn't know that."

"You know some women wear makeup because it gives them confidence."

Shocked by the newly revealed information Chris replied, "Are you serious?"

"Yep, if skillfully applied makeup will often make a woman feel ready to take on the world with confidence. This does not mean that she couldn't be self-assured without the makeup; but it simply serves as a booster to her natural self-confidence."

"So what are you going to do to me?"

China explains in detail as she begins working on each area. "First, I'm gonna apply eyeliner from the outside corner of your eye, stopping two-thirds of the way along the eyelid. When you do this, you should apply with short strokes, drawing the line into the lash line rather than above it. For a more dramatic look, make the outside line a bit thicker than the inside."

"Wow." was all Christina could say in observing China's meticulous attention to detail.

"Next you should set eyeliner with eye shadow by dipping the eye shadow brush into the shadow, and then apply shadow over the eyeliner. This will set the eyeliner, which tends to rub off on the eyelid. Then you need to apply eye shadow to the lower lashes. Using an eye shadow brush, apply the deep-hued eye shadow along the bottom lashes, from the outside in. Unless you have wide-set eyes, don't line the entire lower lid. But instead, stop halfway across, I want to give you a more natural look, so I won't dip the brush into the shadow again, as an alternative, I'm gonna use the excess that's still on the brush for the lower lashes."

"Damn, you got this down to science huh?"

"I took a few classes back in the day and I promised myself after seeing all these hoochies walking around here looking like space raccoons with their multi-colored eyelids I would not be like that."

Chris laughs, "Space raccoon?"

"Yeah you heard me, I mean come on, who in their right mind would wear a neon green dress with matching eye shadow? Eye shadow is supposed to enhance not highlight."

"Yeah, I've seen a few of those girls."

"See Chris, you have nice rusted-copper colored eyes, a smooth even tone and medium brown complexion. Rather than take away from that I'm want to choose a color that is not too much lighter than your skin tone. To me, some people with very dark skin look better with no blush or just a hint so we're gonna add just enough bronzing blush to bring out your strong cheekbones."

Chris seemed to be impressed by China's immense knowledge of make-up.

"Now for your full, luscious lips we want a color that flaunts your complexion therefore we're gonna use deep berry lip liner topped off with a light lip gloss. Yeah, that's it; you know the right lip-gloss when done correctly catches people's eyes making them focus on your best features. And Sweetie, you got all the qualities. In fact you look almost as good as me." She threw out a light-hearted joke, even though there was a very intense look on her face. "Girl, when I get finished with you, you will look even better than me."

That statement spoke volumes to her; for a moment, she could not believe what she was hearing. The very person to whom she had admired, China Peoples would venture to say that Chris looked better than she did. Then she realized that's just how China was always putting others before herself.

"Okay, we're finished, are you ready to see how you look?"

"Yes." Chris said without haste and boiling over with anticipation.

"Here you go." China said as she handed her a mirror and for the first few moments, it was uncertain if Chris liked what she saw for she didn't say a word she just gazed at her reflection.

"Well, what do you think?"

"I don't know who this girl is but, she is beautiful." Chris uttered.

"You know exactly well who she is." China nudges her. "She has been locked in there for years, dying to be released and now that she is free her magnificence will not allow her to be hidden ever again."

As much as she tried, Chris just could not fight back her tears until China gave her a little boost.

"Oh hell nah! After all the time, I just spent on this, you're gonna ruin your make-up by crying?" China said as she reached for a box of tissue. "You better pull your punk-ass together because I'm not going to do this shit again."

Christina promptly regained her composure, stood to her feet and walked over to the full-length mirror on the nearby wall. Her new look, seemed to take full control over her body as her walk was completely altered from its dumpy bounce.

Her head was held high, shoulders rolled back, and she led with her boobs. Her arms swung loosely back and forth while her hips swiveled from side-to-side with her weight more on her heels.

The combination of her symmetrical body alignment and rhythmic movements was sure to send a subliminal message to any onlookers that she was in touch with and in control of her sexuality. Moreover, that would portray beauty, strength, style and elegance.

"Got-damn Girl, where in the hell did that come from?"

Puzzled Chris asked, "What?"

"That walk." China further inquired.

She chuckled at first then answered, "I don't know it just came out like that." She paused for moment in doubt, "Was it too much."

"No, not at all, in fact it was very sexy and provocative at the same time."

"Really?"

"Hell yeah, you look so sultry, I had to check myself there for a moment, because I had the urge to rub myself."

"Girl, you're so silly." Chris said as they both laughed.

"Yeah whatever, look at us sitting around playing while your man is at the law office being seduced by some hoodrat." She said jestingly as she shoved Chris to the door. "Girl, go get your man."

Just then China remembered that there was one more thing that she needed to add to make the package complete. "Chris, wait I forgot something." She shouted.

Chris inquisitively turned around, "What's that?"

"If you gonna look scrumptious then, you must have an aroma that matches we forgot to add sweet perfume."

"You called me back just for that? Is it that crucial?"

"Yes it is, very crucial. Getting a man is just like fishing."

"What the hell are you talking about?" Chris skeptically asked.

China continues, "You heard me, catching a man is just like catching a fish. You have to use the right bait, that has the precise color scheme and with the correct presentation, but most of all you need the right scent."

"Oh, I got that covered." Chris said as she reached into her pursue grabbing a bottle of body mist she purchased from a bath and body shop. However, China completely objected to her using it. "Oh Chris, I know you just didn't pull out that little cheap bottle of $7 body spray."

"What's wrong with it?" She naively asked.

"Huh, it okay if you are going to rob the cradle?"

Still not having any clue what China was talking about Chris probed a little further, "Robbing the cradle?"

"Yeah, that shit is what little high schools girl, wear for their trivial schoolboy crushes. Maxwell 'Mr. Anaconda' is a grown man and to get a man you need to wear something that will grab onto him. Something that is sweet and subtle, yet strong enough to linger in the room long after you are gone. You want him to taste you before he sees you. The perfume that you wear should be so lovely that its flavor smacks his ass in the face and says, "Look at me! But here is the trick, when you depart leave an item behind that has your scent on it, so when he finds it, he'll smell it and it will make him think of you."

"Wow, I didn't know that it was so much to getting a man." Chris said in awe.

"There is and even more work is required to keep him."

"Really?"

"Yes so I'm not going to just send you out there half-ass. Nope, I'm gonna give you some of my favorite perfume."

"And what is that?"

China went over to her vanity, grabbed a long, but thin clear bottle that had a picture of a Poppy flower on it. "Sweetie, this is called *Flower by Kenzo*, it's a very distinct and unique fragrance, here smell."

Chris took a whiff and was blown away, "Ooh, this is nice where did you get this and I like the rose design on the bottle?"

China quickly pulled it back; this is something that I normally don't share with anyone, not even Ivete." She paused gently caressing the bottle, "It's fairly new and only been on the market for about 12 years and that's not a rose it's a Poppy flower."

"A Poppy, what's that?"

"A Poppy is a flower from the Asia." China said as she stepped toward Chris. She sprayed Chris several times, once on her cleavage, once on each side of her neck, and then she grabbed a red scarf from a nearby shelf and sprayed it three times.

"This is what I want you to leave in his office, put it some place where he won't notice it until you're gone."

So off Chris went, but her courage and confidence slowly started to dwindle as she got closer and closer to the gigantic building that lodged the law offices.

If it were not for the guy, she passed at the revolving door, he was so absorbed by how beautiful she looked that he didn't exit, but came back inside for a second look, she would have turned around and went back home.

Every guy she passed eyes were fixated on her and remained until she was out of sight. For once in her life, she felt as though she was the object of desire by all the men and hated on by all the women.

Yes, the women were looking too, but there were no pleasant smiles, flirtatious winks or warm greeting from their twisted faces. The frost from their cold jealous hearts was quite obviously displayed by the callousness of their dirty looks.

It was reminiscent of her college days and when a new girl arrived on campus; everyone wanted answers to the three basic questions. "Who is that?" What's her name?" and "Who is she with?" Except this time, all the attention was on her. The guys at this office building all wanting to know her status with the hopes she is available so they can spit their game or crack on her to get her number. Then on the other side, the women want to know the same, whether or not she is a threat to their current social ranking.

For a fine unattached fresh piece of rabbit in the building could knock one or two of them out of the top 10 ranking. Some were hoping that she was just there visiting one of the many tenants within the building and their spot at the top was not in jeopardy.

This did nothing but heighten Chris's confidence level. "Yeah, you skinny, big head hoes should be nervous." She said to herself as her walk transformed into a full catwalk strut as if she was on a runway at a big New York City fashion show.

Still talking in her head, "That's right all you Hoes, be scared, be very scared."

She purposely stopped to be sure that they all got a look at her flawless new look, "Yeah, that's right you skinny big head heifers consider this payback for every time y'all laughed or made fun of someone large and lovely like me. This is for all my Big & Beautiful Sisters everywhere." She declared silently before continuing with her mission.

Although when she got on the elevator she was subjected to the same adoration and animosity, she did when she first entered the building. To most, this might be a tad bit distressing but she found it to be quite pleasurable. She loved every minute, never before had she been the center of attention.

All the guy's faces inadvertently said 'How you doin this fine day' and the grubby looks from all the women seemed to say 'Oh no, she didn't come in here looking like that.' Nevertheless, she resumed her course on her way to rendezvous with destiny and to get her man.

When she reached the 22nd floor, she exited the elevator into a corridor that had a mirrored ceiling and walls with a solid black marble floor. It seemed that everywhere Christina went she could not help but to see her reflection and reflection of others watching her.

She never had so many men and women freely offer a daily greeting without having to initiate it first. This was new to her it was something that, she could get use to very easily.

"Wow, this is all it takes to get men to notice me?" she said silently to herself.

"All this time, I've been saying this is me take it or leave it, but now I see that the offering had no appeal, well on the visual side. Now it so clear to me, it's not my size that was the issue. The reason why no one took the time to get to know me was all about the packaging. " she continued, "So, I must make myself visually appealing that you are willing to approach me, then once you are there my conversation and intellect will keep you."

"Here let me get that for you, Beautiful." A guy said just as she reached the outer glass door of her destination opening it for her and catching a nice side profile glimpse of her figure eight frame.

Still thinking to herself, "I think it was Mark Twain that said 'Clothes Make the Man' and I wonder if he knew that it also applies to women too? If I had any clue that a little makeover would have this much effect, I would have burned those sweat suits, oversized faded t-shirts and stonewashed jeans a long time ago." She said just before she thanked the man for being such a gentleman.

"I'm never going back to dressing like that again, because what you wear does decide how people perceive you. After all, I've never seen any millionaires wearing raggedy t-shirts. Well except Ted Turner."

Christina entered the office then approached the receptionist who was at her desk. "Hello and welcome to the Law Offices of Hunter, Hines, and Jones, how may I help you?"

"Hello Mary." Christina

Mary looked up with a disgusted look on her face. She didn't have a nameplate on her desk nor did she have a nametag on her suit jacket, so she wondered how this stranger knew her name. Christina, remembered Mary all too well from the difficult time she had during her last visit.

"Hi, are you a client?"

Chris instantly noticed this and took advantage of it, by keeping her answers short. "No."

"Have you been here before?"

"Yes." She replied sharply.

"Do you have an appointment?"

"No." Christina could not believe that Mary was going there with her after all she was there just last night.

Mary became as little irritated by these short answers. "So, what is your reason for stopping by?"

"Look, don't play games with me; you know exactly why I'm here." Chris fired off at her.

Upon hearing that response Mary, face immediately became twisted as she looked at his schedule. "Oh, I'm sorry Mr. Brown is not available at the present time and the earliest I can schedule you for is next Thursday at 8 A.M."

"Don't mess with me you were here when he told me to come by today to pick up the signed document." Chris quickly retorted and wondered if his calendar was really fully booked or was she's doing just as China said she would do, be a *cock-blocking* heifer.

"Okay, I will just try again later." Chris said as she coyly backed away from the desk, taking two steps to the rear then quickly darting past Mary's desk then down the corridor where the offices were.

"Wait Miss, you can't go back there." Mary cried out, as she tried to catch up to her, but it was too late, Chris had already made it Maxwell Brown's office door. Just as Chris began to knock Mary, wedged herself four foot seven, 120-pound frame in between the door and Chris grabbing her by the arm. "Miss, I'm gonna have to ask you to leave the premises now or I will call security."

It was at that time Chris asked herself "W.W.I.D. What Would Ivete Do.?" Within in a few seconds it came to her. "Look Ho, if you don't get your ashy ass hands off me, you won't need to call security. You'll need to call the fire department with the Jaws of Life, to get my foot out your ass."

She followed up this statement with the same psychotic gaze Ivete would give in one of her rare and special moments. In fact, if Ivete were around to witness that whole confrontation, she would have been very proud of how Chris handled herself.

Mary's response however was not one that she expected, instantly her office demeanor went out the window and the real Mary was revealed. "If you feel froggy, then leap bitch."

Just as Chris braced for battle Maxwell walked out, "Is everything okay out here?"

Mary instantly got back into character, "Yes Sir, everything is fine, I was just assisting this young lady," she said in a less aggressive yet soft and proper tone.

Chris on the other hand maintained her assertive posture and spoke clear and decisively, "No what you're been doing is giving me a hard time. I've been trying to get back here to see you, but Miss Thing here has been difficult."

"Ms. Jones, you should have called when you arrived, I would have come downstairs to get you. Come let's go into my office," he said as he led her into his office.

This was not received well by Mary at all and if looks could kill, then the look that she gave Chris screamed bloody murder three times over. Yet, Chris maintained her composure and just gave her the cheesiest of the cheesiest grin in return.

"Now Ms. Jones, how are you doing this fine day?" Maxwell said as he closed the door behind them.

"I'm blessed and highly favored, and you?"

"Well, I can't complain nor can I brag so it would say that I'm doing okay."

"That's good right?" she asked not knowing what to make of that comment.

He laughed, "Yes, it's better than most days, but let's get right down to business. I looked over the contract and I must say I am very impressed, the person who prepared this contract really knows their stuff."

Chris' face lit up like a child on Christmas morning, "Oh that would be me."

"Really? You did all this?"

"Yes."

"Wow, you are just as intelligent as you are beautiful."

"Stop, you're making me blush."

He continued, "If that's what I have to do to get you to smile then, I'm not going to stop. So you are just gonna have to deal with it."

"Mr. Brown you're silly."

"No, I'm serious, you are so beautiful."

"Mr. Brown, let's make a deal?"

"What type of deal?" he skeptically asked.

"Let's past the Sirs, Ms.'s and Mr.'s, okay?"

"Okay, it's a deal, so what shall I call you?" he asked.

She paused in thought for a moment then answered, "Your Highness will do." She said with a straight face.

For a moment, he didn't know how to take that, but it was not until she started laughing that he knew that she was only joking. In her mind, she thought of many names he would be called like Tasty, Delicious and Yummy to name a few.

"Oh so, not only are you stunning and gorgeous, but you're funny too."

She began to blush uncontrollably, "Stop, you're gonna make my cheeks start hurting."

"Well, if your cheeks are hurting from making you smile then, your honor I throw myself on the mercy of the court."

"You throw yourself on the mercy of the court huh?" she teasingly asked and he nodded.

Then seductively she adds, "But, are you ready to pay the fine and serve the time?"

"Yes, I plead guilty on all counts."

"Okay, then I sentence you to taking me to dinner." her boldness came out of nowhere. It had to be the clothes that put her in that mood.

"Oh, punish me, punish me please," he jokingly begged.

They both laughed, "So what do you have a taste for Spanish, Italian, Seafood or Burger King?" he said as he reached for his jacket.

"Ooh Big Spender, you're offering a sister Burger King."

"You know what? I have a feeling that this will be a very interesting outing." He said as they walked out of his office and passed Mary.

"Mary?" Maxwell called out.

Mary quickly jump to her feet "Yes, Mr. Brown?"

"I think I'm gonna call it a day, hold all my messages and move all my appointments back until tomorrow."

"Yes Sir, oh I'm studying for a final exam I have in my law class tomorrow, can I call you if I have a question." She said pryingly, snooping to see if his rendezvous with Christina was over.

"No, I have a feeling that I will be preoccupied the rest of the evening." He said as he looked into Christina's eyes and smiled.

Once again, Mary was not pleased and was almost beside herself when she heard that he would not be available for her nightly call. A call that was nothing more than a scam she used just to have an excuse to call him hoping that things will escalate to the next level.

He didn't mind her calls, as all his evening were spent in front a of an easel with a Hog hair paint brush, a few tubes of oil paint and a tall glass of Beaujolais Noveau. Although this night there would be no easel, no brushes, no paint and most of all no phone call, but boy would there be wine.

Chris and Maxwell got on the elevator and off they went to dinner.

CONFUSION

No matter how hard Nee tried he just could not convince himself that allowing China's mother and Janice to participate in the wedding was a good idea. He just could not accept Deborah's alternate lifestyle. "Damn, I should have stuck to my guns and not given in to China." he said as he drove toward the Blues Note Supper Club to pick-up Tony.

The immeasurable octave-leaping and unique Contralto improvisation of Rachelle Farrell's of Autumn Leaves had a mind-blowing sound that gave him chills. Her voice seemed to molest every scale in the register from the bottom to the top and back down again.

Her voice was so enchanting he lost his thoughts for a few moments, but after regaining them, he continued his rant about China, Deborah and Janice, "It's just plain wrong, a man should be with a woman and a woman should be with a man, no ifs, ands or buts about it."

When Tony called to ask for a ride Nee agreed without hesitation. He knew Tony would see his point of view and support his decision. He sought solidarity with someone who would co-sign on his stern and unyielding stance.

"I know Tony will see this just as I do and said that it is just plain wrong." he reassured himself as he walked into the dimly lit restaurant.

"China, will just have to accept that her mother can be in the ceremony but not her girlfriend and nor can she sit at the family table. They're not married and I don't want to be embarrassed by them being all hugged up and shit." he declared as he stepped to the hostess podium. "If she is to be my wife then she must do just as the vows say honor and obey my wishes."

Just as Nee made that statement, Tony walked up behind him just catching that tail end of his statement. "Now, that's spoken like a man who is about to spend many nights sleeping on a sofa instead of in bed with his wife."

Nee turned around to face him, "What?"

Tony explained, "Bruh, take it from me, if you keep thinking like that you are going to have a very lonely marriage".

"Nah Tony, you got it wrong, man. I ain't gonna stand for that shit, I'm the king of the castle and I rule."

"Nee, I love you like a brother. A dumb and naive brother but still I love ya remember one thing. When she kicks you out, don't come running to me asking if you can crash at my place. You know why?"

"Why Tony?"

"Cause the answer is no, I'm saying it now so I will not have to say it later. The answer is no!"

"No!" Nee asked.

That's right, no and if you don't understand that, I will say in different languages for you in Swahili 'Hapana' in Zulu 'cha', in Arabic 'Laa', in Afrikaans 'Geen' and most of all 'Bu shi zhe yang."

The last set of word confused Nee so, that he looked at Tony with a twisted look on his face. "What was the last one?"

"Bu shi zhe yang? That's Mandarin," Tony answered.

However, Nee's face did not change, so Tony explained it further, "Nee it's Chinese, you see that's why you need to read more to expand yourself".

"But Tony am I your boy?"

"Yeah and—."

"Then why are you going to turn your back on me when I'm in need."

Tony's answer was straight to the point, "I'm your boy do or die when you're in trouble or need but not when your ass is being stupid".

"Whateva man." Nee said with in a hint of disappointment in his voice.

"Brah, I've been telling you since…hell, I can't remember it's been so long, that your stubborn and

151

pigheaded thinking is gonna get you in some deep shit. Some shit that will be way over your head and judging by that comment you just made, it looks like that time is in the near future."

"Nah man, it's not like that."

"Oh really, then why don't you tell me how it is then." Tony said as he gathered his things and heads out the door toward Nee's car and Nee follows."

"Go ahead Lil Brah; I'm listening, what's going to have you sleeping on the sofa on your honeymoon?"

"Fuck that shit; I ain't sleeping nowhere but in my bed."

"Huh, so you think, but let me be the judge of that."

"Okay, let me run it down for you. China wants her lesbo mother and her dyke ass girlfriend to be in my wedding."

Tony paused in disbelief then adding his thoughts, "Nee, I don't mean any harm but…"

Nee interrupted, "Man don't hand me that shit."

"What are you talking about?"

Nee continued, "When people start out by saying 'I don't mean any harm' that's exactly what they do when they say it."

"Okay well, can I ask you a question?"

"Yeah go ahead."

"Are you marrying yourself?"

"What? Man, what kinda dumb ass question is that, of course I'm not marrying myself!" Nee said, as he slammed his car door.

"So you are marrying someone else right?"

Oh boy, here we go with your retarded questioning again."

"Nee, don't get hostile just answer the question."

"Yes, Tony I'm marrying China as if you didn't already know."

"Then it's not just your wedding it's hers too and she should have just as much input as you do. This includes who should or should not be or participate in the wedding."

But, I don't want be to around that type of shit. I don't like it."

"News flash, if you don't like it then you'd better start liking it and getting used to it. Especially if you two plan on having kids, because that person you called a Lesbo will be Grandma to your kids."

This was a revelation and really hit Nee hard, it had not crossed his mind at all.

Tony observed this and added a little more, "Now that Ms. Camille, God rest her soul, is no longer with us Uncle Ty, China, and that Lesbo are the only family you have. So if you don't like her lifestyle you'd better start for the sake of your marriage and your children".

"Man Tony, I thought you would take my side on this, I mean with you being a Muslim and all."

"Muslim? Who told you I was Muslim?"

Puzzled Nee just stared at him for a moment then said, "Wait didn't you tell me that your daddy raised you as a Muslim?"

Tony laughed hysterically, "No, I told you that my dad was buried in a mausoleum. You need to pay attention when people talk to you."

"No, you told me that you were one of those Five Per-centers. "

"See Nee, this proves that you don't listen to half the things I told you. I said that I am one of the five percent of people who believes that there is more to what folks are being told about religion."

"But I've seen you reading the Qur'an."

"So, I read the Bible too it's all about finding out the truth, but forget about me."

"Man, all this time you had me thinking you were a Muslim."

"No, you came to that conclusion on your own; I never said anything to you about my religion."

This was another discouraging discovery that further diminished Nee's hopes that he could find an ally to aide in his campaign against China. He knew his well- disciplined beliefs of Tony's Islamic practice; he would surely side with Nee on the issue that two women living together as a couple was wrong.

Contrary to what Nee thought, Tony's views were nothing as he imagined, "Look Nee, it is not my place to be judge and jury for the action or choices of others. I won't say that her lifestyle is wrong nor will I say it's right. However, I will say that a strong unified family is crucial to the development of the children."

Nee did not like it at all, "Man, I'm not going to have that shit around my kids".

"And why is that?" Skeptically Tony asked.

Nee didn't answer so Tony rephrased the question, "Why don't you want your kids around people that love each other?"

It took a little time but it came out, "Because I don't want that shit to influence my kids".

"Influence your kids how?"

"I don't want them to be gay like them."

Tony chuckled, "Nee, I got some news for you. All the gay people I know have straight parents and I have yet to come across a lesbian, gay, bisexual, or transgender person that has gay parents." Then Tony really went for the knockout punch when he said, "So, it's not the gay folks that make gay babies, its straight parents that are making all these gay babies."

Nee pondered this for a few moments more, "Damn, ain't that some shit."

By this time, they had driven past Tony's street but they were so into their conversation that neither one of them paid attention or even noticed.

"So Nee, you have to be careful about what you say and what you do, because when one throws dirt sometimes the wind blows it back in their face."

"There you go talking in riddles again, now what in the hell is that supposed to mean?"

It means that with all this hatred you have for the gay community you need to be careful how you handle it because God may have it come back on you."

This concerned Nee, "Come back on me how, when it goes against His word it's a sin".

"True some may see it as a sin, but are we all sinners?"

"Yes in a matter of speaking."

"No my naïve little brother, let me educate you on what my reading of the Holy Books has taught me. You see the word 'sin' is such a tiny word, with a lot crammed into its meaning."

Nee interrupted, "Look before you begin, please give me the short version cuz sometimes your ass can be a little long winded. If I'm not cautious it will be midnight and your ass would still be here talkin."

"OK, now can I enlighten your dark closed mind?"

"Yeah go ahead."

"Yeah." Nee said in a less aggressive and subdued tone.

"Nee, can I kick you some knowledge, feed you some Holy knowledge from the *Good Book?*"

Nee became a bit agitated, "Look man, if you don't hurry your ass up, you're gonna finding out *'What Would Jesus Do'* and that's you walking your ass to Jerusalem, when I kick your ass out my car."

"Okay, okay, calm down." Tony said to keep the peace and his seat in Nee's 2002 Honda Odyssey and it was a good thing that he did because saying the wrong thing would surely land him a walk home.

"Now Nee, I'm going to try, but it's going to be hard to say this without sounding too preachy. Let me just throw that disclaimer out now cuz you can be hot-head and short-tempered at times."

Nee now more restless, "Man, just say what you got to say".

Tony starts, "Okay, we all know that Adam the first man, fell to sin, and then sin was entered into the world. Because of his action Adam, introduced sin to the human race."

Nee became a little impatient, "And?"

"Wait let me finish my point. God's forgiveness of our sins and we to live by the commandments of Christ and any sins that we commit through ignorance or weakness can be forgiven by confession in prayer."

Nee shifted his position, his body language gave off the impression that he was not listening but contrary to what his actions said he was taking in every word.

"Brah, each of our sins are not totaled up like exam grades to get a pass or fail. If our sins are, forgiven God remembers them against us no more. If our sins are not forgiven, the grave is our eternal destiny." He pulled out his Bible and turned to the Book of Luke, "See it says its right here, Luke chapter 6, verse 37,

Judge not, and you shall not be judged.
Condemn not, and you shall not be condemned.
Forgive, and you will be forgiven.

"Nee here is where you are going astray; you are judging when it's not your place to judge."

"So what's the point of you telling me all this?" Nee asks.

Tony was shocked to hear Nee ask the question, "Damn Nee have you really been listening to what I have been saying?"

"Yeah and?"

"No have you really been listening?"

"Man, I told you yeah, what else you want me to say."

Tell me that you will let China's mother be in your wedding, If the lifestyle she has chosen is, as you say 'a sin' then it's no greater or no less greater than the sin you're committing by having sex with China and not being married."

Nee became defensive about this then attempted to justify it. "No but that's different…" This time Tony interrupted him, "No sin is greater than the next."

They finally reached Tony's house, after circling the block six times. Now just a few short steps from his front door, Tony felt he had nothing to lose and no longer a reason to bite his tongue. He was home so, if he said something that was offensive enough to get him ejected from Nee's car it would not matter at all.

"Lil Brah, I love ya to death, speaking strictly from my personal experience. You have to learn to pick your battles and learn the meaning of sacrifice and compromise then practice them."

"And if I don't?"

"China will leave your ass faster than a fart in a windstorm!"

"Yeah right!" Nee arrogantly declared.

"Oh, so you're one of those guys that Beyoncé sings about—huh?"

Nee had to ask, "What song is that?"

"Yeah you're one of those guys who thinks they're irreplaceable, but I have news for ya. Your position is not safe not by a long shot."

"Tony man, you're crazy."

"No Nee you're delusional, there is always someone sitting back in the wings waiting for you to drop the ball so they can step in and steal your glory. Some call him the Maintenance Man and others the Clean-up Man."

"That's some of the dumbest shit I ever heard." Nee said in complete denial.

"Say what you want, but he's out there watching how bad another guy treats his wife or girlfriend, waiting for the right moment to approach her.

Nee's conceit went to a completely new level. "Man China ain't gonna fall for that shit."

"Listen Nee, if you're not giving China what she needs mentally, spiritually and physically, it makes her so vulnerable. Therefore, making him come across as so loveable and that's when he starts sweet-talking her. All he needs to do is be nice and lend her an open ear. He tells her and does all the things her man doesn't do any more while slowly building her trust. Then eventually he ends up waxing that ass, receiving gifts at your expense and driving your shit. "

Upon hearing, this Nee's once egotistical posture changed to a disturbed one as Tony went on.

"Someone even made a song about it a few years ago and there is one part of the song the sticks in my head til this day. *'If you don't take care of your business the next man will.'* Then there is the line where he says that the clean-up man *'He can be your brother, father, the mailman, and even your best friend.'*

After hearing Tony's last statement Nee gave him a twisted look. "So what you saying you trying to push up on my girl now?"

Laughing, "No Brah, I'm not into breaking up homes, but China does look good though especially in tight jeans".

"Man, don't be looking at my woman like that what the hell is wrong with you? You are supposed to be my boy and shit."

Tony raised his hands in submission, "I am your Ace to the very end and would not cross you like that."

Letting out a sigh, "Oh okay".

Then with a crooked smile on his face, Tony said, "But I'm not blind either."

Nee gave him a dirty look that he yielded to, "Okay My Brother, let me get out here before you kick me out, thanks for the ride.

"Yeah, whatever." Nee replied.

Tony took two steps then turned around, "Nehemiah, please give some thought about all I said."

Slightly hot under the collar Nee didn't respond he just sped off.

JUBILATION

Maxwell was just what the doctor ordered. Every need and desire Chris had, he seemed to fill three fold. They say at least once in their lifetime every single woman wants to find Mr. Right, but Maxwell was much more, he was Mr. Perfect. He had a good sense of the humor, loved life, and happy all the time, inquisitive, and takes pleasure in simple things.

He wanted the same things out of life as she did and was ambitious, well mannered, and supportive. Just when she thought there was not anything else about him, it totally floored her when he said, "Since we met each morning I wake up I feel like I'm the luckiest man alive."

In essence he was everything that James was not, in fact the contrast between the two were as clear as day versus night. She was beside herself as she shared her thoughts with Ivete when she came into the coffee shop. Ivete was so anxious to hear about how things were going.

"Four years, four long and painful years." Christina declared in disgust. "I wasted being with a man that used and disrespected me." Ivete just shook her head, "I kept trying to tell you, that you could do better but your hard-head ass just would not listen".

Although, Chris did not hear a word that was said, she just kept going on and on about how wonderful Maxwell was to her. "He opens the door for me and oh Girl, he is the first and only man who fastens my seat belt for me." Yet, it didn't matter at all that Christina was not listening to her, this was the happiest she has seen her good friend in a long time. So she just let Christina have her moment, she just sat back watched her face light up every time Maxwell's name was mentioned.

"He convinced me to do it; he is gonna help me follow my longtime dream of opening a Cake Artistry/Bake Shop."

This was shocking for Ivete to hear. How did Maxwell in a few short months what she had been struggling to do for the last 5 years.

Nonetheless, it appears as though the cycle has been broken. As a child, Christina watched as her mother also a full-figured woman had a revolving door of men coming in and out their lives.

Each of them hung around long enough to have a place to stay, get a few meals, the goodies, and then rolling out.

This lead Christina to think that no matter what a man does she must accept it or he will not stick around. She feared being left alone and lonely in her senior years just like her mother.

However, thanks to Maxwell, Christina finally feels like she is worthy enough to be loved. Although they were not officially a couple, she now has tasted succulence of self-worth, respect, and affection. She awoke each morning with a smile on her face and joy in her heart.

It was at that moment that Ivete noticed what Christina was wearing, "Christina, I like that dress is it new?" Christina just smiled and said, "Yes, you like it? Max picked it out for me." Surprised to hear this Ivete, answered, "He did?"

"Yes, can you believe he likes to go shopping with me?" Christina declared as she pranced around modeling the dress as Ivete looked on, "Damn, I've been trying to get you to wear dresses since high school, but you didn't even consider it. Then the idea hit her so Ivete spoke out about it, "That B.B.D. sure changed your mind didn't it?"

Normally, Christina would have a hard time following Ivete's quirky comments, but this time she had no problem. Christina chuckled then said. "Yeah, that Big Black Dick will make a sista do almost anything."

"Oh shit, I was joking when I said that." Overcoming her state of shock Ivete bellowed, "You fucked him didn't you?"

"Now, Vette a true lady doesn't kiss and tell." She tried to downplay it, but Ivete was not having it, "Bitch please you did more than kiss, in fact I can smell the dick on your breathe. Oh my Gawd, you nasty ho! "Christina did not say a word she just smiled devilishly and changed the subject, "So you like my new dress?"

"Nah, you don't get off that easily." Ivete rants, "Your ass is gonna sit down right here and tell me everything and don't skip shit I want to hear all about." Christina facetiously asked, "What, you wanna know where I got the dress?" The Ivete tried to play on her sympathy, "See you don't love me". Puzzled Christina asked, "Now why would you say that?"

"If you loved me you wouldn't put me in a position where I'd have to beat your ass for not sharing with me. Ivete said as her Latin blood began to boil, "You know I'm on probation and the judge told me that if I catch another charge I would have to serve three years locked up in Jessup Prison".

"You see that is your problem Vete, you handle all your problems with aggression and vulgarity." Ivete did not hesitate to retort, "You better get the fuck out of my face with that bullshit, and I ain't fucking aggressive about shit. I'm cool as a motherfucking ice cube and calling me vulgar well that's some motherfucking bullshit too."

Ivete was just being Ivete, and when it came down to it, she knew that there was no harm intended by Ivete's outspoken explicit delivery. Everyone who truly knows Ivete has come to accept that she can be crude and undiplomatic in her delivery but her intentions are good.

"Look Chris, are you going to tell me about your little rendezvous or not? She said with a little more force in her voice, "Because if you're not, then I'll go cuz I got other things that I could be doing."

Not wanting to lose this captive audience, Christina gave in, "Fine, I will tell you, but this shit stays between you and me". She said as she leaned closer to Ivete, "I love China, but at times she has this 'I'm Holier than thou-goody-two-shoes' mentality."

Ivete quickly came to China's defense, "But, you have to understand that China is not just your everyday around the way chick, she gots mad style and she cool with me."

Christina was not expecting anything negative to come out of Ivete's mouth about China, but then again she did not think that Ivete would speak so highly of China either. There was never any bad blood between her two best friends. In fact, she saw it as a blessing, normally there is always a bit of jealousy when two people are friends only because they share the same mutual best friend.

Yet, there was equal love amongst the three of them. "Yeah, I know my two best friends are very special to me and I would not trade them in for anything. Christina replied, "Not even a man, you both are irreplaceable."

"Hold up!" Ivete interrupted. "You may want to take some time to rethink about your last statement and think hard about it." Christina was puzzled by her best friend's proclamation, "Rethink what?"

"Sweetie, I'm gonna let ya know right here and now." Ivete began to break it down for her a little further, "If it came down to a choice of either my girls or some good hard dick...I'm gonna choose that dick every time."

"What? Christina could not believe was she was hearing, "You mean to tell me that you would put some man before your girls?"

Ivete started laughing, "No, not the man, just the hard fat dick that's all." Christina slid her chair back then exclaimed, "You nasty, I can't believe that you would do something like that to your Dawgs. She questioned further, "Where is your loyalty?"

"Where's my loyalty you ask? Ivete sat up and spoke, "My loyalty will be there, right after Mr. Big Dick finishes breaking me off a little sumthin sumthin".

"What about, all that shit you be talking about, huh?" Christina shouted out in disgust. "So, all the dames over dudes bullshit you were talking was just that, just talk right?"

"No, I meant what I said; I will always put my girls before any man."

Feeling a bit relieved Christina loosens her rigid posture. "Now that sounds like my girl." However, Ivete was not quite finished her reasoning, "But that only applies any other time but not today, cuz Mr. Dic-o-luscious is back in town".

"Who Bruce?" Christina went right for the juggler, "Yeah, when that man is around your ass gets soft".

"No I don't."

"Yeah, you do and sometimes I don't know whether to buy you a box of condoms or a box of diapers every time he blows into town."

"I know what the condoms are for and you know I always have him cover up so I won't get pregnant." The she asks. "But why diapers?"

"The diapers are for you." Christina added and Ivete wanted to know more, "Now why in the hell would you buy diapers for me?" Christina quickly replied, "Because when you get around Bruce you get soft as baby shit." Bewildered Ivete asks, "What?"

And Christina obliged, "You become a straight up punk."

"Oh, that's bullshit you don't know what the hell you're talking about."

"Yes I do, it's called being the sprung, dick-whipped, enslaved to the Master Piper, and that's what you are with Bruce."

Ivete refused to admit it, "Girl, you really straight up tripping now".

"Sure I'm tripping just like you're in denial."

"Hey I got to get back to work before China comes in and sees me lounging. Ivete looked around paranoid, "I love her as a friend, but she is a mean ass boss".

Knowing this was nothing more than a way to dodge the issue, "Yeah sure, I have to meet Max anyway". Christina said as she walked away.

Ivete watched as Christina walked toward the door, the temptation to stop her and put all the cards on the table dined on her seared consciousness. For a few details, she neglected to disclose about Maxwell's and her past dealings, made her soul become restless.

Suddenly the thought hit her, what if her little secret was leaked out to Christina from someone other than

Maxwell or herself. If that were to happen the damage would be far greater than expected and the possibility of any sort of reconciliation unlikely. Moreover, what if Maxwell already told her about their past?

Nonetheless, a suppressed secret such as this must be revealed, but delivered in such a way that all the feelings of those involved would be spared. It must also be divulged soon, before the relationship between Christina and Maxwell grows any further. Christina made her way out of the cafe on her way to meet Maxwell at her place, good thing she was well ahead of her schedule because out of nowhere appeared an unexpected visitor.

She heard a voice as someone walked up behind her, "Damn, Christina you look good as shit what did you do get that surgery where they suck all the fat out of your ass or something?"

She stopped dead in her track, "James what are you doing here? " He was shocked to hear a welcome that was hostile and not hospitable, "Well damn, is that anyway to treat your man?"

"My man?" she asked in disbelief as he smiled. "You're not my man anymore you lost that privilege when you did me dirty."

"Come on Baby, don't be like this you know that I love ya." was the only response he could give but Christina was ready for it and had a quick response to his weak reply. "No James, what you call love is not the same thing I call love."

"See there you go again, I see that you've been listening to China and that Dyke-ass Ivete again haven't you." He said sternly then lowering his voice, "Look all I want to do is talk to you."

She put her hand on her hips, "Okay, fine just say what you have to say so you can go, I have things I need to do."

He pointed toward the door, "Can we go inside and talk?"

"No!" ripped from her lips in a firm and unbending tone, "Whatever it is that you have to say you can say it right here."

"Oh, so it's like that huh?"

"Look James you have five minutes, say whatever it is you have to say and leave." she said as she peeked at her watch.

"I miss you Chris and things have not been the same since the day I left."

Without any qualms she said, "Well, I can't say the same, since you left, things have gotten better for me."

"Chris, Imma get straight to the point." He said as he cleared his throat, "I love you, I miss you, and I wanna come home."

"Hell fucking no!" she yelled out before regaining her composure.

He snapped, "Shit is that any way to talk to someone who loves you?"

"No, I mean yes!" she said as her emotions started to cloud her mind and the vivid images of him hitting her played repeatedly in her head. "Let me tell you something James, loving you brought me nothing but pain and misery."

"It wouldn't be that way if you would just do what the hell I tell you to do and stop fucking talking back," he said as the pointed his finger at her.

"You see that's why, I will never let you come back James, if I am your woman you should love, honor and respect me, but instead you want to talk to me like I'm your dog." she said as he stood up right with her head held high. "I was my own woman before I met you, but somewhere in this one-side relationship I lost track of who I was trying to be something that I'm not just for you."

James remained silent; it aroused to see her stand up for herself, so he let her continue. "But never again, I like who I am now and the minute I stopped loving you and started loving me again, the whole world changed."

Not a single word she said sunk in, he was so caught up by how she was standing up without the girls there to back her up or put words in her mouth. In fact, the more she said, the more he became aroused and wanted her.

Rather than making a tactful rebuttal to her last comment, he chose to take a brash and distasteful one. "Why don't you let me come in so you can suck my dick?"

This put Christina in a very dark place yet she still maintained herself, "Okay, on that note this conversation is over, Good-bye James." She said as she turned to insert her key in the lock. As she opened the door, James forced himself and her inside, grabbing Christina by her throat pinning her up against an adjacent wall. "Bitch, don't try to act like you're too good for me, cuz you're not." He moved closer to whisper in her ear, "Your ass belongs to me and when I tell you to do something you fat ass better do it".

There was many a day Ivete would express to Christina that she needed to buy a gun, even if she didn't think she would ever need it. Ivete would preach on many occasions how Christina needed something to defend herself with and the very thing they both feared would one day happen would also came to pass.

Thank goodness, she actually took Ivete's advice and did just that. Within the blink of an eye, James had a Nickel-plated .45 caliber Smith & Wesson pistol shoved into his mouth.

Instantly the tides swiftly shifted, "Oh James let me introduce you to my bodyguard". The newly acquired power that her bodyguard gave Christina was so exhilarating that she began mocking him, "Wai-wai-wai-wai-whi-wait a minute what? Chuckling, "You're not so tough now are you James?" He tried to talk, but the cold, rigidness of the pistol barrel prevented him from properly annunciating properly "Nooooo".

"Huh, I can't hear ya? What did you say?" she asked persistently slowly withdrawing the barrel of the pistol out his mouth.

"No, wait don't do this." he begged. She took great pleasure in this moment, "James, what was it that you wanted me to do?" He hastily responded hoping that she would not remember, "Nothing".

"Oh that's right, you wanted me to suck your dick right?" patronizing him further. "Well, how about you start sucking mine?"

She then started moving her gun in and out of his mouth making him imitate the fine art of Fellatio. "Oh yeah baby, that's it suck it, suck that dick, you bitch." she said as she tormented him further.

Losing all control and power, he lessened his grip and removed his hand from around her throat submitting to her will. "You're not so tough now are you James?" He tried to speak but the bulkiness and movement of the gun going in and out his mouth made his words even more unclear and indistinguishable. Her point now made she pulled the gun out of his mouth and James took off running in the opposite direction.

By the time, she put her gun back in her purse; he was nearly nine houses down the street at the intersection. James was gone; she cleared her head of all the negative energy brought on by James' unexpected visit and opens her front door.

Again and as always, Ivete's little bit of advice prevented another ugly situation from becoming even uglier. Christina contemplated whether she would share this little incident with Ivete. When she ran the scenario in her head, all she could hear was Ivete's obnoxious, and victorious "I told your ass this shit was going to happen" over and over again. "Oh hell no, I ain't gonna tell her ass shit!" she immediately determined.

She looked at the clock on her kitchen wall as she walked in, "Good, I still have enough time to get ready before Max gets here. She locked the door then headed to take a shower and you could bet your last dollar that her bodyguard was still in hands reach as she took her shower.

An hour later her doorbell rang and she dashed toward the door to answer. She opened the door and sure enough, it was Maxwell with a box of groceries in his arms, "Mmmm-mmm-mm!" he said as he gazed at her, unlike any other man, Maxwell started from the top and worked his way down.

Her bangs were still chopped in a semi-circle covering her eyebrows and the rest of her hair was bluntly cut flowing down past her shoulders from an off-center part. Just as it was when they went on their first date. She was wearing a trendy black-shimmer lace overlay, cold shoulder style party dress. This dress was designed so that one shoulder was exposed and a long kimono style sleeve covered the other.

From there his eyes floated tentatively downward hovering for a few moments to admire her tapered waist, curvaceous hips and round wide bottom. When his eyes finally made it to her feet, a pair of black lace, peep toe sling back pumps that had a 6" heel, met them. The height of the heel emphasized the well-defined muscles in her calves, courtesy of spending many agonizing nights at the gym with her personal trainer.

"My, you look so striking in that dress." he said as he gazed at her. "Whoever said, 'one can't improve on perfection' has never laid eyes on you." She blushed from ear to ear then replied, "Why thank you, Max." Then she directed the attention off her to what he was carrying in his arms, "What's all this?"

"Well, I thought that rather than going out to a restaurant, how about we just stay in and I'll cook you dinner?" he answered as she lead him toward the kitchen.

Highly impressed Christina stepped to the side as he began to unpack his bags. No man has ever cared to or even offered to cook anything for her, not even a single piece of toast.

"Really?" blushing even harder that before. "Wow!"

"Yes, all I want you to do tonight Beautiful, is to sit right there and look just as stunning as you are right now."

Upon hearing his last statement, she let out a sigh, "Okay then, I will let you handle your business, and I will run to the little girl's room to freshen up". She headed to the bathroom grabbing her cell phone from of the dining room table on the way. He watched as her hearty bottom bounced out the room, but when she got there, she had other things in mind besides freshening up.

She quickly called China who was woken up from her daily evening nap by Christina's call, "Girl, can you believe this man is over here cooking me dinner?"

China did not seem to be moved by Christina's news, because having a man cook for her was not something that was foreign to her. Nee cooked for her so many times that she has lost count so it was no big deal. "Whoopty Fuckin' Doo for you." China said snide still gathering herself after being torn from her peaceful slumber.

Christina paid China's snidely remark no mind as she went on and on talking. "China, I think tonight is going to be 'the night'."

"The night for what?" China asked. Christina was a bit bashful in her response, "I think tonight is the night I may give him some."

Just then, Maxwell knocked on the door, "Are you okay in there Sweetheart?" Startled she answered back, "Ah yeah, I'm fine; I will be out in a few". Then she whispered to China on the phone, "I gotta go, I'll talk to you later".

China didn't answer she just hung up the phone and turned back over to go back to sleep. "That crazy heffa calling waking me for some bullshit"

Before exiting from the bathroom Christina quickly checked out her appearance in a nearby mirror then tucked her phone behind her back. The aroma of Peach Bourbon met her just as she exited. "Ooh Maxwell, what is that smell?"

"You like?" he asked in a teasing manor. "Yes, what is that?" she asked again.

"Here taste it." He dipped a spoon into one of the pots and fed it to her. When the spoon met her mouth her face lit up, "Oh my Gawd, that tastes so good."

"Its 1/2 cup peach preserves, 2 tablespoons butter, 2 tablespoons bourbon, 1 teaspoon Worcestershire sauce, 1/2 teaspoon dry mustard, 1/2 teaspoon salt and 1/8 teaspoon pepper mixed together into a glaze marinade." he said with a smile.

"Wow Max, that even sounds good." He took her by the hand to give her an idea of what was on the menu. "For the first course we're having my Granny's recipe of mixed greens with apples and strawberries its comprised of fresh salad greens tossed with Granny Smith Apples, caramelized pecans, strawberries, grape tomatoes and crumbled Bleu Cheese, in a Raspberry Vinaigrette."

He paused, giving her time to visually digest the dinner starters, before continuing. "And for the main course, I am preparing Bourbon and Peach-Glazed Pork Tenderloin, which consist of two tender pork loins marinated in a Peach Bourbon Glaze served with fresh harvest green beans and sweet potato hash browns." She was speechless at this point, but he was not quite finished there was still one more dish that he needed to show her.

"And for dessert, we're having Chocolate Truffle Tort." She was so excited she did not give him time to explain before asking, "That sound so delicious what is that?" He answered, "For you, a rich dark chocolate, and a two layer moist cake filled with a delicate and silky smooth Chocolate Mousse fully enrobed in a decadent dark chocolate ganache."

"Wow, you did all this so fast?"

Exaggerating, "Love, you were in for a while."

She knew this meal was full of calories and being on a diet, a meal like this was something that she didn't need. However, she was fearful that if she turned anything down he would be offended. So she approached it tactfully, "Oh Max, all this is too much for just me and besides I'm on a diet."

He turned to her, "Baby, a real man wants a woman that has some substance to her, you know some thickness." he proudly proclaimed. "Only a dog wants a bone, and it's all man right here."

Upon hearing that she smiled, this reiterated the fact that James and Maxwell are complete opposites. Everything that James found disgusting Maxwell found delectable. Maxwell had style, class, and intelligence while James probably couldn't spell intelligence. She loved the fact that Maxwell knows how to treat a lady, and he had a good sense of humor. While James only sees women as objects and if it were not for the change in his pocket, he would not have any sense at all.

"Okay Sweetness, while the food is cooking how about we go into the living room to have a drink." She had to check herself for a moment his presence was so commanding she felt as though they were at his place and not hers. "Yes, I would like that, but I don't have anything to drink but soda and fruit smoothies." He chuckled "No worries, I have that covered." He said as he reached into the box and pulled out a long thin bottle that resembled an olive oil bottle.

Christina saw this and inquired, "Olive oil?" Nevertheless, he corrected her, "No Princess, it's not olive oil; this is Moscato a straw-yellow, sweet white wine." She could see that he was very passionate about his taste in wine because he gave a little bit more than she cared to know. "It's called Moscato d'Asti to be exact with an intensely fruity, aromatic and very persistent edge. Its sweet flavors are perfectly balanced with a low alcoholic content and acidity, which provides the wine with an inviting freshness."

"Wow!" she thought, "All James ever wanted to drink was beer and brown liquor except for that time I talked him into buying some wine for dinner and he came home

177

with some cheap wine that you serve from a box." she giggled, "I bet James tired ass can't even pronounce Moscato."

He grabbed two wine glasses from her counter, embarrassed, she quickly grabbed them from his hands, "Wait those have not be used in a while let me wash them first." She rushed to the sink to wash them, she could feel his eyes they softly caressed every curve of her body.

He took great pleasure watching her bottom as it wiggled and jiggled with ever motion she made scrubbing the glasses. To this day, she still doesn't know what came over or what gave her the courage but out came, "So you like staring as my booty?" Although he was not embarrassed that he was caught he asked, "How did you know?" Her response was short and to the point, "Because, I could feel it getting hot." He smiled then said "Well, I can't help what I like can I?"

She was about to come back with a witty comment, but she remembered the little bit of advice that her grandma told her a long time ago. "Don't give a man too much of yourself too soon. A mysterious woman who keeps a man guessing is a woman that will always have a man after her." That is exactly what she did, but her Nana didn't say she couldn't think about it.

The repressed a comment ran through her mind and that's what slipped out her mouth, "Well Max, if you see something you like, why don't you grab it." Oddly enough, the idea crossed his mind, but he didn't want to offend.

Once the glasses were cleaned Christina's satisfaction they returned to the living room. Max sat down and

Christina put on a little music. "What are you in the mood for?" She asked. I have Eric Benet, Kem, Jill Scott, Ledsi, and Chrisette Michelle and..." Before she could finish running down the list he said, "All of them."

She smiled, "We share the same taste in music I see." He poured her a glass of wine, "Among other things." he said as he handed her the glass after she joined him on the sofa.

She took a small sip from her glass expecting the taste of the Moscato to be just like the other types of wine she tasted before, somewhat bitter and extremely dry. Yet to her surprise it was unlike any other wine she tasted before, "Wow, this is really good." she said elated by the alluring flavor.

He smiled as he took a sip, "Yes, it's appealing and sweet just like you." That comment made her blush, but at the same time, she was slightly skeptical.

"How many women have you done this for?"

He was stunned by this question because it came out of nowhere, but he politely answered. "Not many."

Doubtfully she said, "Come on, you probably have a whole string of women following you home from the club." She jestingly commented.

However, his answer came across very sincere, "No, I don't mix business with my personal life. Mr. Anaconda is a character I created, he is nothing like me, and I like him." He took a sip the continued, "If Ivete did not introduce me to you and I met you in the club, then I would not be here now."

She paused second-guessing her last question hoping that he did not find it offensive. "I'm sorry, it's just I figured with all the other women out here, why does this man want me?"

He leaned closer to her then softly said with conviction, "That's just it you are not like the other women."

This only shifted her mind into overdrive. She was unsure how to take that comment. Was it a compliment or was it a degrading insult? There was only one-way for her to find out so she cautiously asked, "Explain what you mean by that?"

"What I mean is that unlike the other women that I encounter, you don't seem too excited, nor do you seem to be bothered by the fact that I take off my clothes every weekend in front of a bunch of under sexed women." She thought to herself, "Excited, boy please?" as she shifted her position on the sofa. "I'm gonna have to go to the bathroom again, because I'm so wet I don't think my panty shield will hold up much longer." But, she played it cool, not giving him any idea what was running through her head or what was running down her legs.

Then there was a brief moment of uncomfortable silence where it seems they ran out of things to say. Not a word was spoken.

Luckily, the silence was broken when the twang of the guitar solo and the hard baseline of Sade's song "Cherish the Day." The beat seemed to have a hypnotic effect on the two of them, because they both in unison began bobbing their heads head, "Oh that's my girl!" Maxwell said barely able to control himself. "Oh and you have the live version too!"

"Well, I guess this is something else we can add to the list of things we have in common." Christina said blissfully as she joined him in singing the lyrics of Cherish The Day by SADE.

You're ruling the way that I move
And I breathe your air
You only can rescue me
This is my prayer

If you were mine
If you were mine
I wouldn't want to go to heaven

"I have gone to see her each and every time she has come to D.C., Baltimore and Virginia." Maxwell said with enthusiasm.

"You too, I thought I was the only one who was into her like that." Christina said. "Wow, I don't know about you, but for me this is a first, I have never been with anyone who loves Sade as much as I do."

He quickly ceased the opportunity, "Let's make a deal?" he paused waiting for her to acknowledge.

"What's that?"

"Chris, the next time she comes to town let's go see her together."

This made Christina blush even more and she knew that by the end of the night her cheeks were going to be sore from smiling so much. Yet, she didn't care Maxwell had just offered to take her to see Sade when she comes back to town.

She quickly started calculating in her head. "Let's see 'Love Deluxe' was released about two years ago and Sade puts out a new album every 8 to 10 years." Her smile got even bigger, "So if he has set a date with me to go see Sade when she tours again, that means he plans on being around for at least another six years."

"Well?" he asked. "Do I get a yes, no or a maybe?"

She rapidly answered, "Yes, I would like that very much."

"Great!" as he jumped up and ran to the kitchen to check on the meal.

Christina soon followed, "Is everything okay?

"Yes, we're good." he said relieved.

"So you wanna go back to the living room to finish listening to music?"

"Sure, there is nothing like good music and great conversation."

Christina headed back to her sofa and Maxwell followed. Jokingly she commented, "I can feel my ass getting hot again, are you looking at my booty again?" Although, she took immense pleasure in him admiring her plump hourglass shaped figure she was caught off guard when he said, "If I'm looking so much its only because I want to grab it."

"Oh really?"

"Yes really."

"So what's stopping you?" seemed to roll off her lips with such ease that she could not believe that she said it.

He grabbed her by the hand turned her around to face him then wrapped his powerful tree trunk like arms around her waist. That uncomfortable silence revisited them once more, but this time he was ready for it as he slowly leaned forward placing his lips against hers.

Soft, gentle and sweet was the first that thing ran through her mind as she gave back just as much passion as she was receiving. Christina's hands rouse up from her side to his ripped biceps, tracing them up to his shoulders then resting around his neck. This kiss was so scorching that it set her soul a blaze. Never before had a kiss from a man made her feel as though she was not giving enough.

Maxwell thought her voluptuous stature was the right fit in his large burly arms. He felt that her thickness was suitable unlike his many fans that were small and petite. He could hug Christina as tight as he wanted to and not be fearful of breaking her. "Damn you feel so good in my arms," he professed.

This did nothing more than cause her cheeks to hurt even more. "Wow, it feels good to be held like this," she said, as they broke from the embrace and sat close on the sofa. He reached out for her hand as she was willing gave it to him.

He turned her hand over with the palm facing up, "Did I tell you earlier that I used to read people's palms?" Curious she responded, "No really? What does mine say?"

"The first thing you must understand is, I'm a little rusty, I have not done this in a while."

"OK then, what does my hand tell you about me?" she skeptically asked as she extending out her hand.

He gazed at her hand in silence for a few moments. "The lines on your right hand will portray how your personality has changed and what further changes may take place."

Then he reached for her left hand, "If you're left handed, the opposite is true. Now a little impatient, "OK, but what does it say?"

He gazed even harder studying her hand, "Let's see, your ringer finger is longer than your index finger, the greatest space between any of your fingers is between pinky and ring finger." he said as he pointed out each distinguishing feature then continued. "You have an X under your ring finger, a single line under your middle and the longer segment of your pinky in the top. So, this tells me that you would be a great Entrepreneur."

This totally surprised her, not at any time did she every reveal her occupation to him. "Come on, I don't believe this stuff you're telling me all the things that Ivete told you about me."

He quickly answered, "No, she didn't tell me anything."

Doubting him, "Yeah, sure she didn't."

This was not received well by Maxwell so; he let her know exactly what he really saw in her hand. "Oh really?" he said with a little bit of spitefulness in his voice. "Well, do you think that she told me that, you are an affectionate, sympathetic, kind-hearted and compassionate person? You

184

are typically driven by your emotional and intuitive by nature. You fall in love easily and are a passionate, romantic person. Or you have to work harder than most to adjust to new situations and have difficulty dealing with change."

Christina was speechless at this point, but Maxwell just kept going to prove his point. "You are prone to stressing out and worrying too much. You need to be careful not to needlessly over-complicate situations and have difficulty dealing with change, and you are fairly set in your ways." Then he closed by revealing, "You are highly emotional and responsive to others, a humanitarian with idealistic and romantic views of the world. You are capable of being highly erotic and are a very giving lover.'

"Oh damn!" she said very humiliated by all that was extracted from her hand and her life.

Perplexed by her facial express, "Why do you look so disturbed?"

"Disturbed is an understatement try embarrassed."

"Why, when you are no different than the next person." he said. "You are no different than me or anybody else; there is not a single living person that doesn't have their own flaws and short comings to deal with."

"I know it's just that they didn't have theirs put on blast like you just did mine."

To lighten the mood and to get away from the uncomfortable situation he turned to her, "You didn't tell me that you had Me'Shell Ndegeocello's 'Dreadlocks', come on dance with me."

He moved her coffee table aside allowing them enough room to dance. Once again, she found herself clenched in the warm, sanctuary of his arms. "What is this man doing to me?" she asked herself in silence, as she seemed to melt like a Popsicle in Phoenix on the Fourth of July.

"Maxwell?" she asked, "You cook, practice law, know music and you dance, is there anything that you can't do?

He quickly corrected her, "If you and I are gonna spend time together and I hope that will be a lot, you're gonna have to start calling me Max like everyone else."

She craftily responded, "But why, when I'm not like everyone else I'm special, I'm me?"

She waited for a clever reply chuckling, "OK Princess, whatever you want to call me is fine."

Then the silence returned, but this time there was something different. Some strange force compelled her to do something that was totally out of her character. She leaned over to give him another kiss and he openly welcomed it. He gently caressed her cheek with the back of hand. This did nothing more than persuade her to run her hand up under his shirt to fondle his chest.

The febricity of the room roused to a level that was nearly unbearable from their passionate entangled embrace. Stepping completely out of her comfort zone, she mounted him in a full straddle on the sofa. Her breathing now heavier than before and not breaking from their insatiable kiss she began unbuttoning his shirt.

Not worried about anything but losing the moment, "Come let's go into my bed room." she whispered in his ear and off they went.

186

She led him from the living room into her bedroom. As they entered, he quickly turned her around pulling her into his arms and close to his chest. Her 5 foot 11 stature seemed to place her at the right height where there lips could meet effortlessly.

United in a soft deep kiss and embraced in a tight grip. She held on to him so tight, that it would have been hard for him to breakaway if he reconsidered. Although, backing away was the furthest thing from his mind. He held her so tight that if she were of a smaller frame, her ribs would have surely been broken.

Breaking from their kiss, he removed his shirt exposing the inherited body of a Mandingo Warrior. Her hands seemed to be drawn to his strapping arms like magnets as they moved closer. His hands lowered from her waist down to her curvy rear-end grabbing both cheeks pulling them to him. He then turned her around lifting up her hair and zealously kisses her neck. She enjoyed it so much she relieved him of that duty by holding her hair up for him. His hands move down her back flowing up under her arms and around toward the front of her body cupping her shoulders pulling her securely back against him.

Against his body, she could feel what seemed like every inch of his manhood as it became engulf with the heat of the moment and started to swell. It was hard for her to keep still, her panty shield filled to its capacity and began to fail.

Grabbing two heaping handfuls of her voluptuous 44DD breast, he pulled her even closer. She pressed so intimately against his bulging virility she could feel its heartbeat pounding her plushy bottom. Her Powder Puff began to throb uncontrollably in an untamed rhythm making it hard for her to maintain.

Her body took over and her mind followed as she seductively grinds against him. His hands left her breast traveling down under her skirt and up her thigh. He anticipated finding her panty line at her hip, to his surprise nothing was there but flesh. So, he continued up a little higher finally making contact at her waist.

"Ooh my I love high cuts." He said as he continued.

He reached for her waistband his hand gently made contact with her skin, as it continued under her waistband then down to her Goodie Box. Passing it at first, and then returning with an upward stroke, her moistness assisted with his teasing as it transformed what would have been a brisk rub into a light grazing.

She on the other hand, was too deep into the feeling to be embarrassed by how wet she made his hand. Stroking and stroking her pinky-sized love pearl he moved it in a circular motion, which caused her knees to buckle a bit. Gathering herself, she reached back to grab him, to stroke as much of him as she could through his pants.

This aroused him so that he pulled away, dropped his pants exposing his now soaked boxer-briefs. She caught a glimpse of him and was astonished. Although nothing had changed from that faithful night, they met. It caught her by surprise to see Lil Maxwell peeking out from the side of Big Maxwell's briefs. She unzipped her dress letting it fall to the floor.

They faced each other in their undergarments not saying a word. Once again, there was silence. However, unlike before this time it was far from being uncomfortable, it was a welcoming one.

She reached for his hand leading him to the edge of the bed, removed his briefs, sat him down then dropped to her knees.

"Wait!" He said. I am more of a giver then the receiver." He stood up pulling her to her feet, and then turned her around to remove her panties. He put her on the bed on all fours. She thought it was kind odd that he wanted to jump right into it yet, she still complied.

Chris now in the doggy style position he dropped to his knees. Giving her a little tease with his hands before parting her cheeks and then buried his face between her hefty heinie.

"Oh shit! Dayum Baby!" Bellowed from her lips as the aggressiveness of his lapping caused her whole body to shimmy and jiggle that her breasts popped out of her bra.

It did not take long before she reached the point where her toes started to curl and she had to fight to keep her legs from straightening out.

He abruptly stopped, jumped to his feet turned her over onto her back crawled between her legs then resumed dining.

By this time, her juices were flowing freely. He inserted his fingers inside her finding the blissful spot moving them around while sucking her rosy ruby. His fingers were in an area that was unfamiliar to her, yet the way he moved, them had her quivering in a matter of minutes.

189

"Oh Max, oh–oh–oh, that's it right there. "

He sucked in the bulb of her precious flower while simultaneously massaging the very spot that just made her quiver, and then out came a deep earsplitting moan. The intensity of this release took away any control she had left.

Her legs locked his head up like a vise; her body shuttered rapidly like a cell phone on vibrates. She was on the verge of passing out just as her Puffy Almond Joy sprayed all over his face.

D—D–D–D–Don't touch me!" she uttered with a trance like look on her face.

Her body still trembling, she twisted back and forth trying to compose herself enough to make a complete sentence, but no words left her mouth.

The first thing that came to her mind was something was not right something had gone wrong. Then slowly everything that the release robbed her of came back to her as she started to descend from her heavenly like state.

The trembling that once attacked her central nervous system reduced to spasms every three seconds. The violent expulsion of her love juices that sprayed all over his face, now nothing more than a light trickle. The death lock, which held his head now released by a constant rock from side to side, then the power to speak returned to her.

With her senses fully restored, she pulled away and clenched a nearby pillow, "What did you do to me?"

"You just came, you know an orgasm." He answered with patience and understanding.

Nevertheless, a skeptical Christina declared, "No. I know what an orgasm feels like and that was not it."

He clarified, "You had a squirting orgasm, there's a difference you know."

"What?"

"Most women have an orgasm all the time, but not all have a real orgasm."

"Huh?"

He explained further, "Basically there are three types of orgasms a woman can have; the clitoral, the A-spot and a G-spot orgasm." She was still a little confused so he went in to details a little further, "There are certain areas on a woman's body that if stimulated properly can produce a larger orgasm than others."

Relaxed a bit she listens, "Everyone knows about the Clitoris and some may know about the A-spot commonly referred to as hitting the bottom. But, very few get to experience a G-spot orgasm.

He guided her by the hand, "Please trust me on this."

He laid her on her back with her feet flat on the bed; lightly touching her precious pearl then wets his first two fingers before inserting them. Moving them around, gently turning them over to touch her small-ridged mound.

"This is your G-Spot." He said as she tensed up when he pressed it. The more he stroked it the wider her legs opened just like Moses parting The Red Sea.

She was amazed, "How did you do that?"

"Do what?"

"Make my legs open like that."

He laughs, "It's not you or me it's the feeling it produces."

The more he massaged her the more she seemed to sink deeper into the bed.

"Oh shit!" She said as she laid there with her legs fully opened.

"See how good it feels?"

"Ooh yes Baby." She pleaded, "Don't stop!"

"The first time it happens it's a bit shocking, but the more you have it done the pleasure it gives increases also."

He moved a little faster and her body joined in unison matching the rhythm of his fingers. "

"Damn Daddy Pooh yeah, damn!"

He moved faster and faster the closer she got until—.

"Oh shit! Uh, uh, uh,uh! O–o–o–oh sh–sh–i–i–i–it, I'm cum–m–m–m–ming!"

SPLASH!—THE ROOM GOES BLACK.

"Christina? Christina?"

"Are you okay?" He asked as she opens her eyes.

Bewildered, "What happened?"

"You came so hard you passed out."

"Really? How long?"

"Well, do you want to know before or after you started screaming?"

"Wow, it seems like I just keep embarrassing myself."

"Embarrassed? Why would you be embarrassed?" offering her a little comfort. "You just had a very big orgasm; there is nothing to be ashamed of."

His reassurance made her feel at ease, "Wow Maxwell you are something else."

He got up grabbed a hand towel to wash her.

"What are you doing?" she asked.

"I'm about to clean you up."

"Why?"

"Aren't we finished?"

"What about you?" concerned she asked.

"Me what?"

"Don't you want to experience pleasure too?"

"Love, I already have."

"You came?"

He laughed, "No silly, seeing you shake when you came was my pleasure."

"Don't you want to cum?"

"Christina, one thing you're gonna have to learn about me when we're together my needs don't matter just as long as yours are met."

After hearing his kind comment, she tried to keep from blushing but, there was nothing she could to stop it. Not only was Maxwell a smart, sexy and intelligent man, he was one that was not selfish. He was willing to put her needs above his own.

"Thanks, but no thanks, after what you just did to me, I want some revenge." He laughed

"Now put that shit down and get back in bed!" She demanded

"Oh, aggressive are we?"

"That's right I'm not gonna let you come in here and do all these things to me, like calling out the Lord's name in vain then have you roll out on me." she said jokingly. "Nah Brother Man, take off your clothes and lay down."

He silently complied, as she crawled in between his legs grabbing his stiff mast. She used the man sap that it released to aid in making her hand glide up and down his stiffness with ease. The constant thud of his pulse made it jump in her hand as she placed it to her lips. He cringed as the mushroomed tip of little Maxwell disappeared into her warm wet mouth.

Up and down, side to side she moved sending shivers throughout his body. Every stroke she made teased it so, making it thicker and thicker. This also excited her, as her juices were streaming down her legs and her caramel treasure commenced to throb. With his meaty muscle in one hand, she used the other to lift up his bag of jewels to apply a little pressure at its base.

Blood rushed to his already swollen head filling her mouth to the limit of its capacity.

"Em!" She muffled thrilled by what she caused as she withdrew him from her mouth then crawled on top of him until they were face to face.

"Can I kiss you?"

Puzzled by the unusual question he asked, "Why would you ask that?"

"Well, it's just that some men don't want to kiss after having a woman go down on them."

His response was comforting and reassuring, "That's the dumbest thing that I have ever heard. And, for the record, it is mine, I know it's clean and know where it's been. So, I don't have a problem kissing you." He concluded as he pulled her closer to kiss her.

"Wow, I can taste myself on you." She said as they broke from it.

"Oh really?"

"Maxwell, I haven't had that done in so long; I forgot what it tastes like."

Then she mounted his manhood, it seemed to fit snugly between her sweet canal of love and required the weight of her body to drive him deep inside. The blending of their love secretions provided the perfect combination which allowed her to consumed all of his 8 ½ inches of thickness with ease.

"Oh, this feels so good!" she moaned

Caught up in the moment letting the sensation control her pace the velocity of her bounce increase with every downward plunge of her hips. As expected, he reached around clutching her bodacious behind assisting her crusade until she reached a constant but rapid pace.

The continuous meeting of her fully packed bottom against his powerful thighs made a deafening clap that resonated from wall to wall.

As payback for causing her to cum so hard, she wet the bed.

"Okay, time to make him squeal." she said to herself.

She placed her hands on his chest to increase her stride even faster. Like riding a horse in the home stretch of the Kentucky Derby, she rode so hard and so fast the momentum made the headboard of the bed ricochet of the wall. The pace now in overdrive, their breathing synchronized she thrashed her big bottom onto him so ferociously that he could not maintain his cool and collected mannerism.

"Yeah that's it right there! Yeah Baby, right there!" he yelled out."

But just when she thought she had the upper hand, O–o–oh Max, I'm gonna c–um–um–um–um a–ga–a–aaain!"

She quickly rose to her feet crouching over him as her love rained down all over him.

"A–a–a–a–a–aah! O–o–o–oh shit." Exploded from her mouth.

She clasped onto of him and for a few moments, they both laid motionless letting the joys of love making take over their minds and bodies.

Suddenly out of nowhere the words, "Okay, I need to catch up the score is 3 to 0 and I'm losing."

"So, you're keeping score huh?" he asked. "Well, I'm about to get 4 in a few seconds."

After having the most orgasms in one session that she has ever had in her whole life she responded with, "Doubt that."

"Oh really? Let's see about that." He turned her over on her back then joined her in the missionary position, then placed his body on top of her preparing to ease inside.

Although, her body was still recovering she angled herself so she would be comfortable and ready for anything he had in mind. He rose up moving his head down between her dense luscious thighs finding her flooded tunnel of love giving it a few licks before separating its pouty mound.

He used his mouth gently parting her sweet cherry pie, first the left then the right, then taking as much as he could into his warm, moist mouth. Her body responded instantly as short burst of gooey liquid love squirted from her slice of heaven. The sound of his fabulous phallus as it eased in and out of her welcoming mound created a beautiful melody.

Fully within her sugar walls, he turned his torso off to her right side and with her right leg in between both of his legs.

"Oh my God! Oh my God!" She cried out as he continued at a slow gradual tempo. "Damn Baby, you hitting all bottom right now."

"Am I really?"

"Oh yes! Oh yes!"

"Are you okay? You want me to stop." He teased.

She quickly answered, "No, please don't stop!"

Slowly in and out he moved and each inward movement hit its mark.

No more than five minutes in, she began to get in the grove.

Every thrust he made downward was countered by her throwing her pelvis back up at him followed by circular gyrations of her hips. Unlike the first three climaxes where there was buildup, the next eruption crept up on her without warning.

"O–o–o–ooh sh–i–i–it! Oh, shit! A–a–a–aaah!' blazed from her mouth as her body convulsed erratically.

With every contraction she propelled her body upward taking him in deeper until her body was back under her control. She loved how he held her closely throughout the total journey.

"You are one amazing man, Maxwell."

"No, I'm not; I'm just a simple man."

"I'm feeling kinda guilty, I got mine four times and you have not had even one. Don't you want to cum too?"

He paused then spoke, "It takes a lot for me to get there." Then he gazed toward the window, "Most of the time I never get mine, but it's no big deal."

"Wow, that's not good."

"I don't mind, in fact I've gotten used to it, and learned to take pleasure in the total experience rather than a physical release."

"So you mean to tell me that every time we make love there is a good chance that you will not cum?"

"Something like that. Don't get me wrong, I love the feeling associated with an orgasm, but mine are so few and far in between I never think twice about it."

"Then what keeps you going, I've never heard of anything like this before."

"Well look at it this way, most men are finished before she even gets started. But in our case it's the other way around, you'll always get yours before I get mine.'

This was a little disturbing to her, "That may be okay for you but for me it just doesn't cut it. I want to know that the man I am with is satisfied along with me."

"Oh I am, believe me. I got my satisfaction watching your body twitch and tremble that lets me know that, I'm doing my job."

"But Maxwell, what does it take to make you tremble?"

He chucked, "you and me both don't have enough energy that would allow me to get there."

She thought for a few seconds, "What about manually?"

"What, you mean using my hand?"

"Not quite, I mean using my hand, "she answered

This excited him, "I've never had someone do before. I mean outside of work, but that's not intimate and not counting when I do it myself."

"Well, would you be willing to give it a try?"

He smiled, "Sure, I'll give it a shot, but I'm not making any promises."

"Okay." She answered as she headed towards her bathroom and returned with a bottle of baby oil. "Now, I want you to lie back and relax."

She climbed onto the bed straddled him once more, then kissing him from his forehead down to his lips, chin, neck and stopped at his chest. When her tongue reached his right nipple, she lightly licked it then completely engulfed it in her mouth sucking on it. She held it briefly teasing it continuously before moving over to the left. He winced in delight as she allowed him to pop out of her mouth.

Moving lower, she stopped at the mighty beast that had her body convulsing erratically just a few short minutes ago. She grabbed his man staff and gazed at it and all its splendor.

Even though, she had a few private encounters with men in her past, this was the first time she has seen one up close without having it uncomfortably shoved in her face. Unlike the many times with James, this time it was at her leisure.

She examined its shape, which was another first for her. She heard many tales, myths and urban legends about men who had a hooked piece. Even a little bit that slipped out from China; lead her to think that Nee may be the same way.

Until that very moment, she thought all the stories were just a bunch of B.S., but Maxwell was exactly what China and Ivete would call a hook.

Coming to terms with this revelation, she got back to her task. She opened the bottle of oil applying a generous amount on and around his branch then gradually massaged it in until it was bright and glistening like a diamond. Just like a diamond, he was rock hard.

Hand over hand she massaged and kneaded him continuously until his heart raced so fast that it made his meat jump with every beat of his heart. Then she shifted gears, her hands changed from a smooth caress to a full vertical stroke faster and faster.

As the pace of her hand increased so did, his breathing and then he started to moan.

"You like that Baby?" She asked.

"Oh yes." He quickly answers fighting to keep still.

A few twists of her wrist, she alternated her downward strokes with causing him to get closer and closer to her goal until—" Oh yes! O–o–o–oh, o–o–oh." He exploded.

When he reached his plateau, his creamy white milk of passion erupted like a volcano spewing his essence into the air, coming down back onto his shaft and on her hands. She caught a large portion of it and used it as lubrication to aid her in stroking expeditiously creating soft white foam to appear.

Normally she would have stopped but relying on past reports from her girls, she knew this was the time where the head of his warrior of love would be highly sensitive. She kept going causing him to quiver as the foam increased so did the feeling around his *Mr. Good Bar* then— *BOOM!*

He released for second time, yet this time it was much thicker and heavier. In a euphoric state, his body became as stiff and rigid as his man meat and Christina sat in a big puddle of her own extract. Maxwell then quickly sat up, grabbed her by her shoulders and pulled her on top of him giving her the deepest and wettest kiss she had ever had as the night faded away

"Uh shit!" he yelled out. It was so loud that it could have been heard two or three states away.

He awoke the next morning, looked around and Christina had left for work. Beside him was a note.

Maxwell,

Sorry, I could not stay, but I had to meet with a client. Lord knows I did not want to leave the comfort of your arms. I can't tell you how long it's been since; I had someone one holds me all night like I was going to get away. But a girl sure can get addicted to it. I will give you a ring when I'm done, maybe we can do lunch.

Anyway, I wrote this on the whim, I hope you will enjoy my little poem.

I came to you with masked pain.
You showed me a purpose for the rain.
I gave you my sadness,
You returned it with softness
I came to you with chaos
You brought me peace
When I called out in sorrow
You answered with joy
Before you, I dreaded another day
With you, I'm honored while sun sets
and feel cherished when it rises.

Love,
Christina

The night that Maxwell and Christina spent together was a beautiful night filled with many new experiences. There was fire in the bedroom as well as fire in the kitchen as their dinner burned and they had to settle for ordering pizza.

PERPETRATION

Three hours after he left Bruce returned to Ivete's place and she was not too happy, not happy at all. He casually came in and sat down as if it was no big deal.

Ivete on the other hand thought differently, he had been gone for so long it was only right that he spent the first few hours with her. She came over sat down beside him silent for a few moments.

"So, where did you go?" she inquired.

He hesitated for a few moments then answered, "Oh I had to run up the block for a little bit."

"Run up the block for what?" she asked with a little more sternness in her voice.

"I just wanted to see who was still around that's all."

This didn't set well with Ivete, it was one thing to lie, but it was insulting to tell a bullshit lie that had holes in it. While he was gone, she thought long and hard about where their relationship was and where it was going.

"Bruce, you have been gone for three years, there ain't no one up or around that block that should be more important than me."

He sat there in silence as she continued, "You always said that the dudes around here were punks and you'd never hang with them. But no more than an hour of being home you break your fucking neck trying to find them." She quickly jumped to her feet, "Why are you trying to play me?"

The numerous times Bruce came into town on the Northern Wind and left town on the first sign of a Southern Breeze really took their toll on her. The subduing effect that he had on her, normally lasted during his entire visit but not this time around. She was tired of having someone whom she called her man being around half the time. She wanted more from him this time around she wanted him fully, but there was something or maybe someone in the way.

Skeptically she asked, "Then, who was it that you were looking for?" He drew a blank, she was right he'd never hang with the guys in this town. He always said that the D.C. in Washington D.C stood for *Dis-Connected*. No one here was unified; everyone wanted to be a general with no army.

She persisted, "Tell me who Bruce who is it that you just had to see?"

"What?" he asked. "Where is all this coming from?"

"It's coming from me, I want more from you."

"Wait, am I in the right house?" he facetiously asked. "Because, the house I left had a sweet and kind Boricua

Mami in it, not a police interrogator." he said as he stood up.

What brought on this sudden change in Ivete? Was it because she spent so much time around China, witnessing how Nee treated her like a queen? Or was it the passion in Nee's eyes when he looked at China. Maybe, it was because in the far recesses of her mind she knew that when he left her he went to see another woman or possibly a wife.

His actions made it very clear. She should not allow a man who is supposed to be in love with her, just up and suddenly leave town, never to be heard from for up to two maybe three years. Like, he just ran to the store for a pack of smokes.

"Bruce, I want some answers!" she demanded. "And I want them answered today."

"Answers like what?"

Why did he ask that? Every man should know when you are being questioned; you must take control of the conversation. Only provide the information you only need to give, do not let the woman ask detailed questions.

"Where did you go when you left out of here? Who did you see? Was it a female? When you go away for a long period of time where do you go and with whom? Are you seeing somebody else? Are you married? What is her name? Do you love her? Do you have a baby by her?" she asked in session.

See, I told you she asked ten questions in one single breath of air. Amazing isn't it? Bruce made one the biggest mistakes he could make as a man. He underestimated the unique creature that is Woman. Now he has to answer all of the questions and they must all correspond with all the lies and stories he has told her in the past.

Most men lie off the top of their heads; he probably won't remember half of what he told her. That's why most of us prefer to wear sneakers most of the time. There is less of a chance of chipping a tooth, when your foot goes in your mouth with a sneaker rather than a boot or a dress shoe. Oh, well he's on his own on this one.

"Mami, where is all this coming from you didn't seem to have a problem three hours ago when I was rocking your bed," he said in his weak attempt to take her mind off the part of his life that is held from her.

Yet, she was not that easy to distract, "Fuck that shit, and just answer my damn questions."

Bruce you don't have to say it, I'll say it for you. Wait where did the sweet Ivete go?

"I know I didn't fucking stutter Bruce answer me."

Normally, Bruce would not accept anyone talking to him in that manner because doing so usually resulted in gunfire. This time he had to think twice, he knew that she had just as much firepower as he did. And, if everything he taught her sunk in, there were several guns strategically planted all throughout the house at her disposal. Locations that she would not disclose to anyone, not even him, she was a good student.

"Look, I didn't come here to be put on trial like some criminal." She quickly interrupted, "Why are you guilty of something?"

He threw out a little statement he thought would provide some peace, "I came here to spend a little time with someone who I thought loved me."

"But that's just it Bruce, I love you, I love you dearly but not once have I heard you say it back to me...say that you love me, Bruce." She paused in anticipation but did not get what she wanted, "Why can't you tell me that you love me? Is it that you can't because you don't or you won't?"

Yet, he still did not answer her. He just got up gathered his things then headed towards the door. She stepped in front of him just as he reached for the doorknob.

She spoke in a soft but emphatic tone, "Bruce, I'm only going to say this once. If you walk out this door, don't come back." She then re-iterated her proclamation, "If you leave now, I don't ever want to see you again. Don't call, don't write or anything." He paused staring at her with a blank expression on his face.

As always she had to finish on top, she opened the door, "Get your tall bitch ass out of my house and out my life."

He swiftly darted passed her not knowing if she was going to strike him or not, but her words checked him even further, "You walk around here saying that D.C. men ain't shit. Looking at him in disgust, "One thing they have over you is that most are not scared of committing like your punk ass." she then slammed the door.

Not quite satisfied, she opened the door and began to taunt him commenting on his style of clothing, "When you gonna take off that whack ass leather trench?" Then stepping out onto her porch a disgusted look overtook over her face, "You walk around acting all hard, perpetrating and shit, looking like a fake ass Shaft."

She so was so upset that she started cursing at him in English and her native tongue, "You sorry Hijo de puta, I should have left your Culo sucio long time ago. You fucking, Pinche Cabron!"

Trust me these are all words that you and I have either used or heard many times before so there is no need to translate.

Bruce was about 10 miles down the road, but Ivete was still going on, "What the hell was I thinking, taking you back in every time then, you pull one of your little disappearing acts?" Now even more beside herself, "Then you show up out nowhere acting like you never left." She grabbed a bottle of wine from her fridge then poured a hefty serving. "Then just as I get used to having you back, you vanish again and I'm left wondering will it be months or years until I see you again." She gulped the entire glass then poured another. "That lying Bastard probably has a wife and kids."

It was not until a few months later she found out that he was into a little more than what she thought. His unexplained absences were not because he was out spending time with another woman or had another family as China had brought up several times. Bruce was an Enforcer for Tubby Tony of the infamous Russo family. You know the type that is sent out to collect money owed to the Mob.

When Bruce was called in, he would show up with bad intentions, where the only payment that was due always ended up in a few broken bones. Then there were the special situations where someone was mysteriously thrown out a two-story window, causing Bruce to disappear again until the heat cooled down. Yet still, to Ivete it didn't matter, if he could not stick around there was no place for him in her life. She decided that she wants and deserves more just like China and Christina.

Still to Ivete it didn't matter, if he couldn't stay then he needed to go. There was no part-time love here any longer; either you're all in or you're out. Each glass seemed to take her further away the soft and passive Ivete replacing it with the ornery and bitter man-hater we all love. To be honest I don't know if that is a good or bad thing.

"Wait til I tell Chris about this shit she is going to trip." She reached for the phone but stopped, "Oh shit, she is probably out with Max and the last thing I want to do is mess that up. Max is 1000 times better and more of a man than that punk ass James." She clinches her teeth, "Damn, I can't stand that man". She then corrects herself, "No, calling him a man is giving him too much credit.

Ivete was on the money, Christina was out with Max, and she was having the time of her life. Their original plans were to go check out the latest Tyler Perry movie but he surprised her with an impromptu picnic at Rock Creek Park.

He went all out; he arrived an hour early to set things up, found a nice spot that had the right balance of sunny and shade. He had speakers attached to his MP3 player playing music to set the mood. There was a bottle of wine on ice with two glasses and container of fresh cut strawberries and pineapple slices placed neatly on a plaid blank.

Ironically, just as they approached the song A Long Walk by Jill Scott began to play. This was the first thing that Christina noticed. The lyrics "Let's take a long walk in the park" and being that they were walking in the park kind of gave her the chills.

Max lead her up to the blanket and she took a seat and he sat down beside her but facing the opposite direction.

"So, do you like?" he asked.

"Yes, I do! She quickly answered, "This is really nice, and no one has ever gone through so much trouble for me before."

"Believe me when I tell you this is no trouble." he replied as he handed her a glass of wine. "Let's toast to the beginning of a wonderful friendship."

She raised her glass but inside she was thinking as she looked at him hungrily, "Friendship? Man, what I want to do with you is not something that people who are just friends do."

He felt just as she did but, did not want to come across as being to forward. His eyes wondered down her plump and hearty thighs stopping midway just above her knees where they peeked put from her shorts. He loved the way the sunlight glistened off her skin.

Under normal circumstances, she would have been self-conscious about a man staring at her legs but not today and not this man. She wanted him to look, stare and gawk at her thickness. She went so far as to put on an extra layer of Vaseline before leaving put, just to be sure that at any given moment her legs would look sexy and smooth.

He noticed that she saw where his eyes went, so it swiftly apologized. "Please forgive me if I stare, it's just that I find you so appealing."

Christina's face lit up like a firecracker on the Fourth of July. No man has ever looked at her lustfully before, but more than that had the style, class and respect enough for women to feel compelled to apologize for doing it.

She found herself asking him that old cliché' "Where have you been all my life?"

He just chuckled but she was serious.

"Max, I know it's only been a couple of weeks but no man has ever made me feel this special." She said as she grabbed his hand, "And I want to thank you."

"Thank me for what?" he said confused, "You're thanking me for treating you like the queen that you are?" He took a sip of wine then continued, "Feels kinda funny you thanking me for treating you the only way I know how."

It was at that very moment, she stared to second-guessed herself. Did she give it up to him too soon? Timing was everything, giving up the goods prematurely may lead a man to think she's too easy then he'll bounce. Making him wait for it and hold out too long, he may get frustrated and still bounce.

This was something that was so delicate; she would have to seek guidance and advice from her girls; China and Ivete. She knew China would tell her all the right things to do and Ivete well, would tell her all the wrong things to do.

Therefore, she would do exactly what China says and do the opposite of whatever Ivete tells her. But then again, she saw how his attentiveness toward her had not withered; in fact, it appeared as though it increased. Therefore, it was not worth bringing it up to the girls.

Max had Christina wrapped not once, not twice but three times around his finger, she lived off his attentiveness. Max on the other hand was drawn to her sweet innocent nature and unlike all the other women; she didn't look at him as a sexual object but a man of substance. He was a good man that was worthy of the love of a good woman such as herself.

"I want you to taste something," he said as he reached pass her.

Christina was feeling him so much her horns went up and her mind instantly dipped straight into the gutter. However, it was abruptly redirected when he came back with a container of strawberries.

"Try these," he said as he lifted one up to her lips.

She took a small bite and instantly her eyes lit up,"Mmmmm, that is so good, what did you do to it?"

He smiled, "They're Strawberries soaked in Chocolate Vodka."

"I know about strawberries but I've never heard of Chocolate Vodka."

"Really?" she asked.

"Huh, all James ever drank was malt liquor and Hennessy."

"James, who is this James?"

At that moment, she could have kicked herself. She broke one of the key rules of dating after a break up. You should never bring up your ex on a date unless you are asked and if are you are asked, keep it short and sweet. Saying negative things about your ex is bad but saying good things is even worst.

"Oh, James is my ex."

"Well, if James was really all that, he would be sitting across from you now instead of me right?"

"True."

"Do you still have feelings for him?

Without any hesitation she answered, "No."

Good! He's not here so I don't need to hear any more about him. Cool?"

Max's sternness in putting Christina in her place did nothing but make her want him even more. After all most women love a man that can take charge. However, know that some of you will disagree, but don't shoot the messenger. I'm just telling the story, not writing it. So, your beef is with the author and not me. Anyway, back to the story.

The rest of the picnic went on without any real issues. Christina mentioned James' name just three more times, but Max as patient as he was overlooked it.

They departed just as the sun was starting to set. It looked like a bright Florida orange ready to be peeled as it slowly crept out of site behind the horizon.

"Max, please don't take this the wrong way, but I'm not ready to go home."

A bit puzzled, "What makes you think I would take it the wrong way?"

"I don't know," she said now feeling a little silly for saying it.

Nevertheless, Max being as smooth as he was knew just what to say, "I was thinking the same thing." This brought a smile to Christina's face.

"Tell you what let's freshen up and the go to a bar or something." he said as he opened her door.

"That sounds like a good idea and I know just the place," she said.

The Blues Note was the only place that came to her mind. She knew that if that place was able to create some fond memories for Nee and China then maybe it could do the same for her and Max.

This place is one the most well thought out themed dinner club I have ever seen. It's not surprising at all that it's always a long wait before you are seated. Imagine this; you walk into a dimly lit restaurant the Maître d approaches in a canary yellow pinstriped Zoot suit with a matching yellow hat. You know those suits with the wide baggy legged trousers, worn high on the waist with tight cuffs at the ankles. In addition, the jackets that are so long, they come pass your knees with exaggerated shoulder pads and wide lapels.

Finishing it off with a classic wide brim felt hat with a long feather and a watch and chain that hangs down to the knee. Oh and I forgot the Spatz or wingtip shoes. You folks born in the 60's should know what I'm talking about but those who don't have any idea, Google "Cab Calloway Zoot suit."

There he asks, "What's your pleasure?" No, get your mind out the gutter, keep in mind this is a classy 4-star restaurant. When he asks, what's your pleasure he is referring to the tables. There are five dining areas name after a few of the legends of jazz.

Oh, I forget to mention, unlike other establishments, The Blues Note, dance floor is in the middle surrounded by all the sunken dining areas. Each of the five dining areas are uniquely sectioned off. When you walk in, to your immediate right on the edge of the dance floor is Coltrane's Corner. It's named after the mind-blowing saxophonist John Coltrane. Coltrane's corner is filled with red plush crescent moon shaped booths that have glass-topped tables perched on top of four silver saxophones fused together at the base. The glass of each tabletop rested on the necks and mouthpieces of the sourly horns as each faced outward.

The walls were also red with many small yellow marks in somewhat of an abstract pattern. This was specifically designed to mirror his patented rapid-fire improvisations and his bold cathartic wails done like no has ever done before. Last, there was a large black and white photo of the man himself looking down at the patrons of the area dedicated in his honor.

As you continue through Coltrane's Corner, further back on the right, you will reach Parker's Pit derived from another great saxophonist Charlie Parker. Unlike Coltrane's Corner, the booths and tables were "V" shaped with blue plushy seats. The tables were held up by brass colored saxophones in the same manner as Coltrane's Corner.

The walls here were painted white in a pattern that resembled a chicken's feathers, aimed to represent his nickname Yardbird. Also on each table were three vases filled with blue water that substance a white floating candle in each. This characterized his emotional expressiveness with the instrument that left the audience gasping for air.

At the rear of the right side was Miles' Mountain, which sat a little higher than the other two areas on that side, overlooking the entire room, named after the world-renowned trumpeter Miles Davis. Here there were tables and booths of different shapes and sizes, each had its own scheme depending on how many they could seat. The walls were black and the basic colors of the tables and chairs were black, cherry brown and burgundy.

This area never stays the same you could be there one day then come back the next and everything would have been rearranged. All this was to exemplify, Miles at his prime, the embodiment of a restless spirit, always thrusting himself and his music into unchartered waters.

Coming back to the front on the left side, you would find two instead of three dining areas. You would also be in for a long wait, for these are the most popular areas in the establishment. Only those who are fortunate enough to be seated there are led down to a little footbridge that carries you over a three-foot wide channel of water. The other side houses Dizzy's Delta a diamond shaped platform-dining area.

As you would assume this is named after unrivaled trumpeter Dizzy Gillespie. Here you are surrounded on four sides by a canal of water boxed in by safety rails fashioned like bridge supports. Just like at the entrance to Dizzy's there is a similar bridge at the rear that connects to the next dining area.

Dizzy's Delta has more of a contemporary modular decor, it's as if the owner purchased all of the furniture from somewhere like Ikea. All the tables and chairs were high bar stool style made of Philippine Mahogany and each had different pictures of the man himself transposed on them. The goal the owner had in mind with Dizzy's was to display his improvising on chord changes in a song and how he introduced new chord changes based on the song's melody.

Once you've passed through Dizzy's, and if you were smart enough to make reservations, you'll have the distinct pleasure of getting a table at Ella's Island the unofficial VIP area.

Following the theme of honoring the legends of jazz, where the other areas pay homage to all male horn players. It only seems right that your best area should be dedicated to the first lady of jazz, the flawless Ella Fitzgerald the singer's singer. Her control is sure, her notes are clear and her pitch is precise. Her rhythm is impeccable. She was truly a gifted, one-of-a-kind, once in a lifetime unique talent.

The same body of water that surrounded Dizzy's Delta encompassed Ella's Island. Although slightly higher than Dizzy's it also was the largest area in the whole venue. It was the size of Parker's Pit and Miles Maintain combined.

It has a round stage that was encased by draped white lace curtains that flowed from a large chandelier down to the safety railing and then down to the floor.

The tables were covered with white table clothes and arranged to accommodate two per table. This area provides a romantic yet elegant setting and specifically designed with a little bit of privacy from the other areas. It was not surprising that this was Nee's favorite spot and why China loved him so, because any man that brought a lady here would definitely score major points.

Maxwell's was comparable to Nee in the romance department so, Christina knew that he would love dinner at the Blues Notes on Ella's Island. Over the years, she heard of many complex plots and strategies women used to hook a man and until now, she thought they were all elaborate exaggerations. Yet, she found it very amusing that she was orchestrating one of those very intricate plots.

Max thought going to the Blues Note was right up his alley, a nice place to sit and continue to explore each other.

"Sweetheart, that sounds like a good idea."

At that moment, all she could do was smile, "Did he just call me Sweetheart?"

Upon hearing that, she quickly grabbed her phone to put in an emergency call to China, hoping that Nee was with her. If he was, she was going to ask him for a big favor. You see Nee's best friend Tony is a waiter there and she was hoping that he could slip her name on the waiting list for Ella's Island.

Within a matter of seconds Christina had China on the line, "China, where is Nee?"

China didn't take well to not being greeted appropriately by one of her girls and it was even more disturbing that she asked for her man. "Hello Christina." China said in a very sarcastic tone.

"Girl, I ain't got time for your antics, where is Nee?"

Still wanting to be acknowledged, China continued her sauciness "How are you doing today, Christina?"

"Girl, don't play with me, I need to talk to Nee right way."

Sensing the urgency in her voice China passes the phone to Nee. "Hey Christina was going on?"

"Nee, I need you to do me a big favor."

"Sure, what is it?"

"I know that it's short notice but can you see if Tony can get me a table at the Blue Notes?"

"Is that all?" chuckling. "That should not be a problem. Actually now is a good time to go. They're adding several Giant Koi to the pond today and shutting down for a couple hours."

"Really, that's great thank you."

"Not a problem at all, I'll give him a call and tell him to give you my table."

"Nee, thank you oh so much."

So, after a quick phone call, within a few minutes Max and Christina were on Ella's Island at the Blues Note, having a great time. Well, until James showed up.

ALTERCATION

A few days after their last confrontation, China began making the final arrangements for her big day. Now one would think with Nee having a change of heart allowing China's mother to participate in the wedding, it would be smooth sailing from this point on.....right? Nope, smooth was something that was far, far from the truth.

Nee and China were on the same page on how they wanted simple a wedding, China's mother and her girlfriend however, had gone off the deep end. It seemed that everyone had their own opinion of how they thought her wedding should be but no one cared to hear what the bride had to say.

China was in a bad predicament, every time she tried to speak up, someone would talk over her. It got to be too overwhelming for her so, when the time was right she made a beeline for the door. She needed to seek refuge and she needed to get it quickly.

221

Yep, its times like this when you call on the one person who is your rock, the foundation of your existence, your partner, your heart. You call on the one person who no matter what the situation always has your back.

Although, this was a problem that she dare not take to Nee. If he knew this was going on, that someone was taking advantage of his Babygirl. He would go off, letting everyone in the immediate area and maybe four doors down would hear him clearly. You can mess with his car, his money and anything else he owns, but if you mess with his Babygirl then you going to have to deal with Hurricane Nehemiah.

Okay, venting to Nee was definitely not an option. Therefore, when you can't go to your man with your problems, you go to the next best thing. She knew that Christina was probably out with Max, it's been so long since she had a real man in her life, she dare not spoil her groove. That left Ivete as her next choice, calling her was something that she thought over very carefully before acting on it.

She knew that calling Ivete would be a conversation filled with a plethora of "you should do this and you should do that's" instead of lending a sympathetic ear.

"Oh what the hell, I'll let her get it out of her system first, and then maybe I could get her to understand my point of view." She said as she dialed Ivete's number.

"Hello" Ivete answered in a gloomy tone. China immediately keyed in on this, "Damn Girl, what's wrong with you?"

"Bruce is gone." she replied.

"So what else is new?" China naively said, not knowing the specifics of the occurrences at 3939 Nathan Way earlier that day.

"No, this time he's gone for good, I told him not to come back."

"What?" China asked as she heard the shocking news.

"Yeah, I told him that if he was not going to stay then he should leave and never come back."

"Wow!" was all that China could say and at that moment her problem became insignificant. She knew how much Bruce meant to Ivete and helping her get through this difficult time took priority. "Are you okay? Concerned China asked, "Do you need me to come over there?"

"Nah, I'll be okay."

That's what came out of her mouth but her tone said something that was contrary to that. "Look, I'm on my way over there." China said not giving her anytime to retort. Something such as this was not something that a real friend would take lightly. Ivete had always dropped whatever she was doing to come to the rescue of Christina and China, thus it only seemed right that they were there for her.

China invoked a Code 13, of the Sister Support System or SSS. This is code is only used in extreme situations such as this one. When this is put into play everyone drops what she's doing and rushes over to the one is trouble. Everything that was going whether good or bad was put on hold, even Max.

China calls Christina who was over at Maxwell's apartment curled up watch movie, "Chris, Code 13 at Ivete's place."

Christina was stunned the emergency code was placed into effect, "Why? What's going on?"

"Bruce is gone."

This did not surprise Christina at all, "Is that it?" She said she said a little perplexed. "What else is new?"

"No Chris, this time it's for good, she told him not to come back."

Christina quickly leaped up off Maxwell's chest "Say no more I'm on my way."

Concerned by the urgency of the phone he just heard, "Sweetie, is everything okay?"

"Yes and no, it's just that one of my girls has a little crisis and she needs me." She didn't specify which one of the two; it was being that she didn't know how much he knew about Ivete's love life. "I'm sorry Baby; I have to leave you so suddenly."

"No, no, no you don't have to apologize, that's your friend, and she needs you," he said as he followed her to the door. "Far be it for me, to come between you and your girls."

"Thanks for being so understanding, come here." she said as she gave him a peck good bye then turned toward the door.

He then grabbed her by the arm pulling her back into his massive arms. "If you have to leave me so suddenly, let me give you a real good reason to come back."

He then proceeded to give her a deep passionate kiss. It was so sensual it made the small traces of hair on her arms stand up. This was unlike any other kiss she ever had before because when they broke from the kiss she was breathless. Maxwell then said, "If that kiss was not enough to make you wanna hurry back, then how about this." He ripped off his t-shirt exposing a finely developed body that resembled that of LL Cool J or 50 Cent.

"Got damn!" burst from her lips before she could catch it from coming out. He just smiled with delight, "I'm glad to see my point hit home."

She blushed in embarrassment. No, it wasn't exactly from her verbal outburst but from his comment as it conjured up the devious thought of, "Yeah, I would love for your point to hit home." cascaded through her mind.

"Let me go now because the more I sit here looking at you the more I want to stay."

"Okay, but if it's not too late when you're done, you can always come back." he said as she continued out the door.

She turned around to get one last look at that fine piece of chestnut colored man candy, shook her head then mumble, "Lord please, have some mercy on a sista." Then she continued on her way to meet up with China.

Within no time they were at Ivete's place, they used their key to open the door. "Vette, we're here." Christina called out. "Where is she?" China asked she searched from room to room. Yet, Ivete was nowhere to be found, they heard rustle at the door and she walked in.

Startled to find both her girls there, "Hey, what are you guys doing here." China was even more surprised by Ivete's entrance. "I called a Code 13 because you broke up with Bruce, I thought you needed us." Ivete laughed and said,

"Chris, tell China what I say is the best way to get over a man."

Christina was not happy to quote Ivete, "The best way to get over a man is to get under one." Ivete then piggybacked off Christina, "That's right; I don't need y'all to help me get over a man. All I need is a big dick fat dick and I will be fine."

China was appalled by her statement, "That's just downright nasty if you ask me." Ivete's response was curt and to the point, "Well, nobody asked you so you can keep your opinion to yourself." If someone else said this to China, it would have been on like grandma's stove Sunday morning cooking grits. However, that's the type of answers we have all come to expect from Ivete, anything less would be a strong indication that something is wrong.

"China she's fine let's go." Christina said without hesitation. China was amazed at how Christina quickly lost all concern for Ivete's plight so she sarcastically asked, "Oh I'm sorry Christina are we keeping you?" Christina quickly answered, "Yes." China did not expect to receive such an immediate answer, but when she did she questioned it, "So, what is more important than one of your girls in need of support?"

"Girl, it is plain to see that Ivete is fine and she doesn't need us." Christina said as she gathered her belongings, "You called saying there was a crisis so, I dropped everything that I was doing and rushed over leaving a big black half naked man home alone. Now that we see that everything is fine, I wanna get back to my big black dick, I mean man."

China was completely thrown by Christina's brash and bold statement. If someone else told her that Christina made such an outlandish statement like that, she would not believe a single word. "Who are you and what did you do with Chris?" China asked. Christina laughed, "What are you talking about?" China looked over at Ivete, "We need to call a priest, The Men in Black or something because something has taking over this girl."

"No, she is just coming into her own. This is the person who she is supposed to be and not the person everyone wants her to be," Ivete proclaim with pride. "That's right Chris; fuck what everyone else thinks do you." "Thanks Vette, hopefully I can link back up with Max to salvage the rest of the evening." Christina said as he headed toward the door.

China waited until Christina was out the door, "So, you still haven't told her about you and Max?" This question put Ivete on edge, "No, I haven't." China let out a big sigh, "You know the longer you wait the harder it's going to be, and the harder it's going to hit her." At that moment, Ivete's voice took on a melancholy tone, "Yeah, I know." China on the other hand remained diligent, "How much longer are you gonna wait, until they get married and have children?" she said as she walked out the door.

In her track to reconnect with Max, Christina receives a call from the one person she never wanted to hear from again, James. "What's up with you? He asked as she answered his call. She was very short with her answers, "Not much."

He acted as if nothing happened between them. "I been thinking about you and I miss you, I know you miss me" She could not believe that he had the audacity to even ask if she missed him. "Are you serious?" she asked then became caustic, "Oh yeah, I miss you just like I miss the beatings, the cheating and the weed smoking."

"Nah, baby it aint like that at all, I've changed." he replied trying to sound sincere but Christina was not falling for it. "You and I know damn well, the only thing you miss, is me financially supporting your all your bad habits."

He did not take too well to her cutting remarks, "Bitch, don't you talk to me like that, I'll beat your ass." Unlike many of his furious outbursts, she was prepared for this one. "Just like I thought James, nothing has changed with you and we have nothing more to talk about." He noticed that her will was a lot stronger than before. "I see that you've been letting that Lesbo put shit in your head again." She just blew him off, "Whatever James." and hung up the phone.

She did not realize that he'd been following her for the last seven days. In the eyes of the law, this type of action is referred to as stalking, but if you called him out on it he would say he's just checking up on her. If Christina knew he was following her, she would have done everything in her power not to lead him to Max's house. Only if she discovered this before she departed Ivete's, but now it was too late she had already reached her destination.

She parked her car in the parking lot and proceeded to Max's building but had her happiness stripped when James ran up behind her. "Hey you." Christina looked as if she had seen a ghost, "James what the hell are you doing here?" Christina asked. His smile had just as much deception to it as his reason for being there. "I was stopping by to see an old friend."

She believed him about as much as she believed Tupac, Biggie Smalls and Elvis were going on tour together. "Oh really, you are visiting someone? Who?"

He did not answer at first he needed time to think. "Um, I-I-I-I came to see F-F-Freddie." "James you're lying" Caught like a weasel in a hen house after sundown, yet he was relentless, "Mary, I swear to God, I'm not lying to you."

Christina's ears started to burn, as if they were doused with gasoline and set afire. Her keys dug deep into the flesh of her hand as it closed tightly around them. "I know you didn't just call me some other girl's name." He resorted to the patented PDS method. "What?" Unyielding she clarified, "You just called me one of your nasty ass hussy's name." "No, I didn't."

"Yes you did, you called me Mary."

"You tripin, I don't even know a Mary, there you go again trying to start some shit."

She realized continuing such back and forth banter delayed her from the reason she was there and it had nothing to do with James or Mary. "Okay James, whatever." she said as she took a step forward to pass him, but he blocked her path. "Where is all this 'Whatever' shit coming from?" She did not respond sidestepping him continuing her mission.

James on the other had something else in mind, "Bitch, don't fucking walk away from me when I'm talking to you," he said as he grabbed her by the arm. She turned giving him a look that had so much heat it could lit a match.

She leaned close to him and in a calm yet cool tone said, "Make that your last time calling me a bitch, or else your ribs won't be the only thing hurting, OK?"

The two of them stood there facing each other like two gladiator squaring off before battle.

Their intense glaze was broken only by a man's voice as he approached, "Sweetheart is everything okay?"

Max embraced her giving her a passionate kiss then turned placing his body in between the two facing James, "Do we have a problem?" James stepped back changing his offensive stance, "Nah, we cool." James replied cowardly not looking Max in the eyes as a man should. Christina fought to keep from smiling; it was refreshing as a cool rain shower on a hot summer's day. Never before had she ever experienced the reassuring comfort of being defended and not attacked by the man in her life.

"I'm Brown, Maxwell Brown and you are." he said extending out his hand. James' voice acquired a less balking manner almost a feminine modulation. "James." His response astonished Christina it's not like James to give just a one-word answer to anything. Maybe he was changing and there was hope for him after all. She started to regret putting him in this predicament. "Max, come on lets go inside." She grabbed his hand leading him away. James watched as they walked away then got into his car and drove off.

The rest of the evening went without any other incidents. Maxwell and Christina enjoyed each other's company until the early hours of the morning. Christina awoke finding herself nestled comfortably a top of Maxwell's broad chest.

"Damn, I can get use to this." she said to herself as she got herself together. Maxwell got up after her looking over at the clock, "Is it too late or too early."

Christina laughed, "That depends, if you are just getting in its too late and too early if you're like us just getting up."

"Can I use your bathroom before I head out?" He led her toward the bathroom, "Sure it's right here." She scuffed across the floor as the pressure from her full bladder intensified. She forcefully closed the door behind her ripping down her panties seeking relief. "Man, this feels so good she mumbled."

When she exited he was standing right by the door, "Oh My God, I hope he didn't hear what I was doing." ran through her mind. He stepped aside allowing her to pass, "Wow, you really had to go, huh?"

Christina's complexion was normally a shade lighter than a freshly brewed pot of coffee, but changed to the same color as Merlot wine, when he revealed to her that he heard every single drop.

He seemed unfazed by it; after all, it is a natural bodily function. She lowered her head, "I'm so embarrassed." He reassured her, "Come on, it's not that serious." This did provide some comfort but a true lady never lets her guard down.

On the way to her car, James who popped out from behind two parked cars approached her. "Oh so it's like that huh?" Christina came close to jumping out of her skin, "James, what the hell are you doing here?" He started to stutter again, which meant only one thing he was lying. "I-I-I just got back; Greg and I are going to play golf today."

She knew this was far from the truth; it was hard for her to believe that both of James' friends lived in the lived in the same complex as Maxwell. "James you're lying, you don't play golf." He made a poor effort to cover it up, "Yes I do." The fact that he did not admit that he was lying did nothing but piss her off, so she interrogated him further.

Notice, I said interrogate and not questions. I say this because when a woman suspects that a man is lying, she begins a line of questioning which only serves one purpose. Her goal is to trip him up on his lies. I know you've seen those police shows like CSI or Law and Order, where they have the bad guy sitting as they throw question after question at them. Golf was something that she had quite a bit of knowledge about her dad was an avid golfer, and as a child, she spent many days as his caddy. "James you're playing golf?" she asked.

"Ye-ye-yeah."

"What's your handicap?"

"Huh?"

"What does it mean when you have an Eagle?"

"Huh?"

"Have you ever had a Mulligan?"

All these were basic terms that anyone who has played the game should know if they were really playing golf.

"Can I see your clubs?"

"Ah, I don't have any Wayne and I share his clubs."

By this time, she was convinced that he was lying but to be sure, she threw out a baited hook. "So this Wayne is the same person you came to see last night?"

"Ah yeah why?" he asked stupefied.

"Hah, I knew you were lying because last night you told me that you were here to see Freddie and then you said you were here for Greg but now you're telling me it's Wayne. So which is it?"

Refusing to be caught, "They are all the same."

"James that's bullshit and you know it. There is no one named Freddie Greg Wayne."

James confessed before she got too far away, "I saw you leaving Ivete's house, so I followed you. I wanted to see you and I knew you wouldn't answer my calls."

Christina found this confession to be flattering and disturbing at the same time yet did not show or give any indication of such as she got into her car and drove off. It was not until she was well into her journey when the effects of James' words take their toll.

As much as she enjoyed spending time with Maxwell, she still had a soft spot for the old James. The James that was displayed just before she drove off, the man whose arrogance, pride and everything else took a backseat and had no place in their relationship. Did James finally wake up and realize his harmful ways?

CONFRONTATION

No matter how much Ivete tried to avoid it the subject just kept popping up. There was no way around it, she had to tell Christina about the past that she had with Maxwell. Something that needed to be done quickly turned into something that must be done. Each day that passed, Christina's feelings for Maxwell grew deeper and stronger. She was so into Maxwell, that it was not if it was going to hurt her, but how much.

Ivete met with Maxwell that morning at the local McDonald's to discuss a plan of action. "Wait, you hooked us up and you didn't tell her that you and I been together?" he asked.

"I didn't think it was important at the time and I had no idea you two would hit it off this well." Concerned he inquires further, "So, she has no idea what went on between you and I?"

Ivete embarrassed answered, "Not a clue."

Her answer made him sick to his stomach. He too had profound feelings for Christina and thought things were going well for them. He had no idea that his past with Ivete would come back to haunt him and weigh heavily on the present as well as the future.

Ivete looked toward Maxwell. "So, Max what are we going to do?"

He sighed, "I have no choice but to tell her."

Ivete interjects, "Just like that? You think it's that easy?"

He replied without hesitation, "Yes, either she will accept it and understand what I did or who I did before her has nothing to do with the here and now."

"Answered like a typical male." Ivete responded.

"You men, really fuck my head up with you just add water bullshit quick fix answers." Her response knocked him for a loop, "What is that supposed to mean?" She rolled her eyes around in her head, "Men are such dogs, y'all think that it's okay for you to fuck around with a girl your boy has been with, but with us women it something different."

He didn't take kindly to being generalized with other men, "So, is that what you think of me, a dog like the others?"

She promptly addressed this, "No, that's not what I meant."

Giving her every opportunity to dig a deeper ditch or get herself out of one, "Then, what exactly did you mean?"

She answered, "Unlike men, women have an unwritten code of ethics and the number one rule is that all ex's are off limits."

He interrupted, "That is the dumbest thing I have ever heard and it doesn't make any sense."

"Of course, it doesn't make sense to you because you are a male, but to us females it makes a lot of sense. So you and I being together means that Christina and I, are not supposed to happen?"

Mentally dissecting what he just heard pushed him over the edge, "You and your girl code can both go to hell. From what she tells me about her past, this the happiest she has been in a long time and no silly little code is going to prevent me from giving her that happiness." He gathered his things, "Look, she and I have dinner plans tomorrow at eight, so you have until then to tell her about us. If, you haven't told her by that time I will." He then walked off.

This time constraint did nothing more but add to the existing pressure that Ivete felt. Avoiding the issue was no longer a luxury she had. Therefore, rather than continue to let this demon further haunt her, she called Christina.

"Hey girl, you got time to talk?" Christina replied, "Yeah, sure what's up.?" Taking a big sigh, "I need to talk to you in person; can you meet me at the coffee shop in about 30 minutes?"

"Sure, Vete is everything okay?" shaken by the distress in Ivete's voice.

"I will tell you when I see you." was the only answer Ivete gave in calm, but not reassuring tone.

Yet, when she got off the phone, her stomach knotted up so, it felt three times as bad as monthly cramps. Her breathing was as though she just ran a marathon. Sweat oozed from her palms they were so clammy her cell phone popped out of her hands and bounced across the floor. Her ears burned as if the sun had beamed on them all day with no shade. Steam exploded from her olive color of face like ice cold water being tossed on a hot grill when it met the blistering chill of a 50 degree Northeastern Breeze. Unfazed Ivete continued on her trek to meet with Christina. In her head, all the possible scenarios played out and not one had a happy ending.

"Damn, I should have told her about me and Max that night when after her gave her that lap dance." Then a second thought hit her, "For as long as I've known him, I have never seen Maxwell go that far with anyone, not even me."

It never crossed her mind until that very moment, "That would be instantly attracted to Christina from the very moment he saw her." This explained why he reacted so severely, when he found out Ivete did not tell Christina about their intimate past.

The long 20 minute drive it took to go from the McDonald's to the coffee shop seemed as if it were only two minutes as Ivete's stomach began to twisted and turned, knotting up tighter than a virgin's Va-ja-ja. Being a control freak, it was always situations where she did not have any control, that she felt the most uncomfortable. Procrastination once a reliable ally helping her avoid reality, now became her feral nemesis, dominated her mind, body and soul.

"How did I get myself in to this?" said asked herself as she entered the storefront. She surveyed the area and to her dismay there were only two customers in the shop, a couple in the corner gathering their belongings set to depart. "Anyway, there goes my safety net." she hoped that there would be customers there because if there were people around diminished the likelihood of Christina causing a scene.

Out of desperation, she approached the waiter, "Excuse me, I'm a good friend of China can you tell her that Ivete is here?" Her stomach churned even more when the waitress said, "You just missed her, and she had an appointment and will not be back for another hour or so."

Ivete fought to keep her knees from buckling the waitress noticed then asked, "Are you okay, can I get you anything?" There was no answer so she asked again, "Miss, is there something I can get you?'

Ivete's olive colored skin rapidly turned four shades lighter and the pupils of her greenish-gray colored eyes began to dilate, which alarmed the waitress.

"Miss, are you okay? She said as she led her to a table, "Maybe you need to sit down." Ivete still did not say a word, "You, just sit right there." The waitress said as she swiftly walked to the back to get some water. The whole ordeal was getting the best of her, never before has someone else's feelings mattered that much to her. So much that she was on the verge of having an anxiety attack.

Something like this normally would not get even a small flutter from her cold heart, but this time it was different. For once, she really cared about hurting someone else, worried that such a short and insignificant relationship of the past would haunt her today.

Repeating herself again, "I should have told her about me and Max before they got serious. At the very least, it would have given her the choice to continue to see him or break away clean. Nonetheless, she put Christina in a bad predicament breaking The Girl Code.

For those who don't know, although it's not written anywhere. The number one rule for all women, is that each girlfriend is forbidden from hooking up, kissing, dating, and/or screwing any of her other girlfriends men. This includes every guy she has been interested in, or shown interest in her, from the age of 13 until she or he dies period! Failure to do so will lead to a serious beat down and banishing of said friend from the *Inner Circle*.

Ivete tried to rationalize, "Who made up these dumb girls rules anyway. After all, they are your ex for a reason and sometimes for only a season." She tried to talk herself into believing all that she said. "This is one of those stupid rules that is outlandishly dumb and should be stricken from the list of over the top rules"

It was at that moment her fear got the best of her; completely out of character, she grabbed her things and made a break for the door. "I can't do this face-to-face she's gonna have to hear the bad news by phone." She sighed in relief making her way out the door, but in no more than two steps of her size seven feet she heard.

"Hey Girl, where ya going I thought you wanted to talk to talk me."

Her heart skipped a beat as she turned around and her voice, which is normally a mild baritone, was now an extremely high-pitched soprano. "Oh there you are I thought you got caught up and traffic so I said I would catch up to you later." Ivete quickly replied.

Christina looked at her with a strange look, "Girl, what's going on with you? You know darn well, there is no traffic this time of the day"

Her escape foiled, there were no other options, but to just tell Christina everything. She headed back to the table where she sat no more than thirty seconds ago, "Sweetie, sit down I need to tell you know something about Max."

Puzzled about what Ivete could possibly need to tell her about Max, that he didn't already tell her himself. He led her to believe that he had shared everything there is to know about him in his own way. It was what he called his Open Book Policy, but maybe he didn't open his book wide enough or to the right pages.

In the back of her mind, Christina knew that there had to be something wrong with Maxwell; he appeared to be too perfect. She convinced herself that maybe it was something like an illegitimate child, which was something that could be worked out between them. They spent a lot of time together and his cell phone never rang so he couldn't be involved with someone else. There was no way it could be anything more than that and the thought of him having another women or being married definitely didn't cross her mind.

Then her mind began to wonder. "Does he have a disease or something? What is it? Is it contagious?" She asked as curiosity began to consume her. Ivete didn't realize that the more she delayed telling her the more Christina wanted to know. "Ivete, you know how I don't like to play these games, either you're gonna tell me or not?"

Ivete let out a big sigh before continuing, "Chris, I never told you how Max and I actually know each other."

Christina added, "Yeah, it did cross my mind, you and I have been tight since high school and you never mentioned him until that night in the club. So I suppose that is what this is about...huh?"

"Yeah Ivete replied in a humbled tone that immediately set off alarms in Christina's head." Ivete, please don't tell me you met him while you were locked up."

Ivete corrected her, "Locked up? All the charges that were pinned on me were dropped and ruled self-defense; I have never spent more than 24 hours in jail."

Christina questioning her further, "Then is he someone who you met while in court?"

"What are you trying to say Chris?" She asked but did not get a response. "Is that what you think, all I associate with are thugs and criminal?"

Christina didn't want to go there but she went for it anyway, "You know, Bruce isn't exactly a Baptist bishop."

"Wait a minute Chris, I know your big ass aint sitting over there talking about the character of my ex, when your ex wasn't shit, aint shit, and will never be shit." Ivete fired back.

Christina quickly retorted, "Then James is just like the Underground Railroad now, a piece of Black History. I have a good man now, Max and unlike James, he takes care of me in and out the bedroom.

Still simmering over what Christina tried to imply about Bruce made it easier for Ivete to drop the bomb. "Oh, you don't have to tell me how good Max is in the bedroom, because we used to fuck all the time."

Just then, Christina felt like she had been smacked in the face with a cinder block. How could you do this to me was conveyed from her eyes. Her eyes that began to fill to their capacity with tears like two hazel colored balloons about to burst. Ivete was too consumed with malice, too far in her zone to notice that she just ripped out her best friend's heart and defecated all over it.

Still stunned, Christina sluggishly and lugubriously got up then walked out without saying a word. No more than 20 seconds later, remorse invaded Ivete's heart expelling all of the wickedness and evil that compelled her to deliver the destructive news in such a cruel manner. Although this was not how she wanted to break it to Christina, she did not have to carry it any longer, the weight of this burden lifted. Then her mind shifted toward the damage that was caused to her sister.

She thought that once she told Christina the secret, she would feel a lot better but that was far from the truth. In hindsight she felt even worst, her best friend had found her prince charming but a dark cloud of deceit ruined her happily ever after. Her next step was to get out of the cafe before China returned or else she would never hear the end of it.

Christina felt betrayed and bewildered, she could not understand how Ivete could do this to her. So many thoughts ran through her mind at once that she developed a headache.

So many questions that needed answers ran through her head, "Was Maxwell really into her as he appeared to be or was he just doing Ivete a favor and pretending to be all that she needed? Why was this information withheld from me? Was this done out of pity? Can I really be involved with a man that my best friend knows intimately? Was their little fling completely over or were there still some residual feelings that could easily rekindle? Could they be left alone? And the most important question, would she be forced to choose?"

Upon leaving the cafe, Ivete called Maxwell to inform him that she broke the news to Christina. "Okay, I told her." She said remorsefully.

After a brief silence, he asked, "How did she take it?"

Letting out a big sigh, "Not well, not well at all."

"Maybe I should give her a call?" He stated.

"No!" Ivete lashed out. "I don't think that is a good idea at least not now. Give her some time to herself."

Yeah, I think you're right" he said in hindsight.

"Hey I got another call; hit me up after you talk to her." She said as she switched over. On the other line was a livid China. "Vette, I just spent the last hour on this damn phone trying to talk Chris out of whooping on your ass."

"Yeah right, if she even dreamt about putting her hands on me she' d better wake the fuck up before I turn the dream into a motherfucking nightmare."

243

"Damn Vette, even when you're dead wrong you still don't show any compassion."

Ivete came back in full swing, "What are you talking about, I have a lot of fucking empathy."

China astonished by her crude response, "Girl, do you really listen to yourself when you talk? To me that is not the tone of someone who is sorry. I bet I have more empathy in my pinky finger than you have in your whole body."

Not knowing how to respond Ivete just fired back, "I don't give a fuck"

"Whoa Bitch, you need to check you caller id so you know who you're talking to, because I ain't the one. Your ass ain't but a hop skip and a jump away from me. Talk to me like that again and I'm gonna be all over that ass. I'm not saying I will win, but your ass will know that you been in a fight." Then China regained her composure, "Look, you and Chris are my girls and I'm only trying to help you two work this out."

Not backing down Ivete detoured away from a confrontation, "So you wanted me to tell her and I did. Now she's hurt and I understand that, but there is nothing I can do about it now."

"Wow Ivete, you're a real nutcase."

"Damn China, what did I do now?"

"Ivete, you just don't get it do you?"

"Get what?"

China realized there was no way Ivete had the kindness or the sensitivity it took to make this wrong right. "You are hot headed, rude, obnoxious, have no tact and most of the time you can be a down right bitch."

All this was something that she knew about herself so there was no harm done by China speaking so freely so she allowed China to proceed without interruption. "With all that being said, there is another side of you that is for lack of a better word loving. Loving in your own sick and demented kinda way, but once you get in a zone there is no escaping your wrath, which is harsh when dealing with others. However, that type of stance just doesn't work with those who you care about and care about you."

Then Ivete interrupted, "What day is it?"

This question came from left field leaving China a little bewildered, but she answered it anyway. "Tuesday why?"

"Tuesday huh, can we save the sermon from Sunday Morning?" She replied coyly.

"You see that is exactly the bullshit I'm talking about, you don't give a damn who you hurt, all you care about is you come out on top."

Quickly denying it, "Oh com-on that's not true."

"Oh yeah? So, tell me how did Christina react when you apologized for hurting her?" Ivete didn't say a word and China rubbed her nose in it just like one would discipline a puppy for peeing on the carpet. "See, you don't really care about her, it's all about you."

Her demeanor become a little less hostile, "That's not true I do care about her."

China continues, "No you don't because if you did you would not have put her in this type of situation nor would you have let her walk off without apologizing to her. She is your best friend and treats you like a sister but you can't say the same? You need to make things right and until you do, don't even think about calling me." China hung up the phone.

Her heart now heavy and filled with guilt Ivete sat motionless pondering the situation at hand. "Is what China said true? Am I that selfish?"

Meanwhile, clear across town, Christina took a long walk in the park to sort out her thoughts and feelings. She had a big decision to make a decision that would probably affect her for the rest of her life. The Pro was that she found a real man that treated her like a queen. The con was he withheld vital information from her and although, he didn't lie, he wasn't exactly forthcoming with the information either.

When they went out on the town, he made her the envy of all the other ladies, making her the headlining topic that consumed the remained of their evening. "How did someone as big as she is, get someone like him?"

He was everything to her a friend, confidant, lover, a rock and now a deceiver. Even more, the fact that he had been intimately involved with her best friend, and not disclose this fact, really made her question if any and everything she loved about him was real and true.

Then on the other side of the coin, was her girl, road dog, her ace boon coon. To which they pledged that they would never let any man come between them, the *Divine My Chicks Before Dicks Sisterhood*. Christina found it extremely hard to be upset with Ivete. She was so in-debt to Ivete. If it were not for Ivete, I don't know where I would be. "She has always been there in my time of need rescuing me from any crisis.

Ivete was always there to pick her up when she was feeling down and to fight all her battles. There were so many instances where she saved Christina from being badly beaten by James. There was many a day where Ivete sent James home with a broken nose and a few black eyes. There was even one time when she locked him up in a rear naked choke and had it on him so tight that he blacked-out.

Oddly enough, most of the assault charges filed against Ivete were because she was defending Christina. Actually, it's hard to say if Ivete did, things like that, because she loved Christina that much or loved to fight more. However, at that moment, it didn't matter because Ivete had betrayed her best friend. A friend that she had a long history with and at the very least, an apology should have been given.

This one neglected act made it so easy for Christina to hold a grudge against her best friend. "Why should I be loyal to her yellow ass when she can't do the same for me?

The more she thought about it the more she became angry, and then her phone rang. She answered without checking the number, "Hello."

"Hey how are you?" The voice at the other end asked.

"I'm blessed and highly favored" was the only answer she could give despite her current plight; she instantly recognized the caller's voice.

"I was wondering if you and I could go somewhere and talk." The caller said.

She didn't say anything at first then replied, "Ah okay, when and where?"

"How about your place in an hour?" The caller said with delight in his voice.

"OK my place in an hour."

"Great, see you then beautiful."

When she got off the phone, she felt renewed as though her dilemma did not exist. She got up and gingerly walked toward her home.

Exactly one hour later there was a knock at her door, she answered it and there he was. In a warm welcoming voice, she said, "Come in"

He eagerly walked in as he passed her she noticed that he had put a lot of effort into dressing for this little talk they were to have.

"Wow, I've never seen you like this, you look so dapper when you clean up." She said with smile.

"Thank you, it's just a little something, something I had in the back of my closet."

As they proceeded to her living room, she looked him over a second time. "And you shaved too, wow!"

He sat down, "Yeah, well something's change and in fact I've changed. That's what I wanted talk to you about."

Astonished, "Really?"

"Yeah, Chris, I'm so sorry for what happened and I really miss you and I want you to give me another chance."

Pausing for a moment, taking the time to choose her words carefully, "I hear what you are saying, but how I do know something like that will not happen again?"

He plead his case with sincerity, "What happened in the past is done, over and we can't change it. It is what it was and so shall it be."

She was highly impressed by his profound statement, "Wow, you put a lot of thought into this didn't you?"

"That's right, like I said I've changed the old James is no more. You're looking at the new and improved James."

Christina didn't know what to make of this so-called New James. Although, on the outside it appeared the he changed but somewhere inside she knew the old James was still lurking, just waiting to come out.

Her optimist side led her to believe that maybe he did change for the good.

The time couldn't have been any better, the messy situation with Ivete made it so Maxwell may be out of the picture, so there was room and time for James. "So can I get you anything?" Humbly she asked.

"How about one of those glasses of Muskeato, you're always drinking?"

She chuckled, "Do you mean Moscato?"

"Yeah that's the one." He answered.

She was a little leery about giving him alcohol, knowing that it may lead to trouble but then again this would give her an opportunity to see if there was a future with him.

She went to the kitchen to get the glasses leaving her phone behind on the table in front of him. It was on vibrate so there was no way she could have heard from the kitchen when it rang. It continued to ring for five rings then stopped; it rang again five more times and stopped. After the third time it rang, James grabbed it to check the number. He was surprised to see that the phone was not locked.

It was always locked when they were together so this made it even more intriguing to have access to her phone. He knew that it would take her a little longer to get the bottle opened, so he had ample time to go through her phone. He first checked the call-log, to see who felt it was so important to reach her that they called three times back-to-back.

"Maxwell Brown? Who is this bama?" he asked silently as he scrolled down the call-log. Reaching the 30th call, he stopped counting. Then he started to view her photo album finding an album titled "My Love". In it were many pictures of Maxwell by himself and some with the both of them hugged up together at the Blues Note.

Upon this discovery, the room began to dilate, the air was dry and stale, his heart launched to sprint nearly bouncing off the inner wall of his chest. His nostrils flared, his jaw clenched grinding his teeth together. All of which was like an evil incantation that awakened that ugly green-eyed beast we all know as jealousy.

When she returned and had no clue what transpired while she was out of the room. "Okay, here ya go one glass of Musketo." His pleasant, kind and reformed charade was instantly dropped, "I know your big ass is not trying to make fun of me? "Wow, the new you is a little on the sensitive side I see. I'm sorry if I offended you." She said trying to keep the peace.

After all, the things he viewed in her phone he felt that being tactful and charming was no longer an option. So he got straight to the point. "Look, I wanna come back home. So whoever you're seeing now you need to cut it short."

She did not take too well to him telling her what she had to do. Even more, she was convinced that James moving back in so soon was not a good move. She still had to feel him out and make sure that all the things he had told her about his change was real and he was being sincere.

"James, I'm happy that you have begun a new journey in your life by changing, but I don't think that you moving back in so soon are a good idea," she said as she got up from the sofa. "So for right now the answer is no. I need more time, we need more time."

He got up and followed her, "What do you need more time for? We already know everything about each other."

She countered, "Exactly, that's why I want more time; I want to be sure that this is not a scheme you came up with to get your foot back in the door. She turned to face him, "Point blank, either we do it my way or we don't do it at all. He took a step closer with his fist clenched; she saw this and said, "You know what? On second thought, I say let's just be friends."

James didn't handle being rejected well, instantly he resorted back to his old ways. The abusive monster she knew him to be. He threw the wine glass to the floor breaking it, and then grabbed her by her throat shoving her against the wall. "If I can't have you then no one will." he said as he pulled out a pocketknife then placed it close to her neck.

However, unlike many times before, she showed no fear. She looked him directly in his eyes, "What are you gonna do James kill me?" She grabbed his hand pulling the knife closer to her throat. "Go ahead James, do it! I'd rather die than be in an abusive relationship again."

Her voice changed from a stern one to one of compassion, "A man is supposed to love and honor his woman as he loves and honors himself. You see, God made her of him and not for him." She felt a little relief from his grip as she continued, "A woman is not his property to be commanded nor owned. She is a part of him; his rib, she, and he together are of one flesh. James at first I thought, you robbed me of my self-esteem, my self-respect and my dignity. But then I realized that you didn't do anything to me that I didn't allow you to do."

She released her hold on his hand before continuing, "All I wanted was to be loved by someone, because I couldn't love myself."

This struck a nerve with him, his tightly rigid body also became somewhat relaxed as she resumed, "And the sad thing is you are just like me, you can't love anyone because you can't love yourself."

She closed her eyes, took her last breath, and uttered. "If, I have to choose between being in a loveless relationship or death, then go ahead and kill me."

This declaration left James dumbfounded, the lady that stood before him was not the same women he controlled and dominated. She had strength, pride, and overflowed with self-esteem. He backed off removed the knife from her neck lowered his head and walked out not saying a word.

Relieved, that she was no longer in danger yet proud that she stood her ground. Her hand shook uncontrollably as she reached for her glass taking a sip hoping to calm her nerves. It was more evident now that Maxwell was the one for her.

Despite, not revealing his past with Ivete, she felt it was not enough to keep her from happiness. Thinking now more rational, "Why am I buggin out over this? The Maxwell and Ivete thing had to be over because she never spoke about him at all. He only recently came up and out of nowhere. Since we started dating all of his evenings were spent with me and not Ivete."

Now a bit more reassured, "Besides, if there was something still going on between those two and Bruce found out about it, Maxwell would have come up missing a long time ago." Then her thoughts shifted towards her relationship with Ivete. "Why am I tripping? She has been my girl for many years and I have never heard or known her to deal with a man who has someone else. "

It was really started to sink in that she may be making a big mistake, "Nah, not Ivete! If a guy that was involved in another woman ever tried to push-up on her, she would not have it. In fact she would tell him to kiss her ass." After putting things into prospective, "What was I thinking, the only thing she did wrong was not telling me from the beginning that she and Max had a thing."

She analyzed the situation a bit further, "Wow, I was about to throw away everything my best friend, my love and my chance at happiness." Then without any further thought, she grabbed her phone to call Ivete. After several rings she got Ivete's voice mail, "Hey Vette, it's Chris we need to make things right, give me a call or stop by when you get a chance, Love you, Bye!"

She added the "Love you" to give Ivete a hint that there were still l cool. After hanging up from that call she called Maxwell who answered on the third ring. Again, with tenderness, "Hey Babe, can you come over so we can talk and to try putt this behind us and move forward."

He was so relieved to hear that she didn't want to throw in the towel and walk out on them. She could hear the enthusiasm in his voice, "Oh yes, I will be right over.

Not more than 30 minutes after she got off the phone, she heard two voices yelling outside her house. She ignored it until the voices got louder and louder, so she casually glanced out her window to investigate. She was shocked when she got to the window to see Maxwell and James engaged in an argument. She knew that under normal circumstance James would not have had the heart or the nerve to stand toe to toe with another man. He was a coward, unless he felt he had the upper hand, an equalizer such as a knife.

She quickly ran towards the door and down the stairs of her porch to intervene, just as she made it to the last step. James pulled out his knife stepped back and thrust it three times into Maxwell chest.

"No!" she screamed as Maxwell dropped to his knees as James ran off.

Rushing over to Maxwell who was lying in a pool of his own blood, "Oh no, Lord Jesus!" she said hysterically rolling him over onto her lap. The ruckus drew a crowd as all of the neighbors exited their homes. "Someone call 911!" she tearfully shrieked.

Looking up at her and in a weakened raspy voice he said, "I-I-I'm so sorry, please forgive me." Pausing to catch his breath before resuming, "For not telling you about me and Ivete."

"Baby don't, that's not important right now." She begged using her hands in a failed attempt to stop the blood for pouring out of his limp body as sirens off in the in distance grew louder and louder.

It didn't take long for the news of the stabbing, to reach Ivete. She rushed to the hospital to find a blood covered Christina sitting in the waiting room dazed in a trance like state. Although, there were ties to both Christina and Maxwell, her only concern was her girl, her best friend.

"Sweetie, are you okay?" grabbing and hugging her.

Still staring out in the voided space, she began to speak, "Max is...is gone." she then broke down crying.

"Oh Sweetie, I'm so sorry." She professed allowing the sympathy and compassion for her friend in need of comforting to take precedence over her desire for rage.

"Love does not delight in evil,
but rejoices with the truth.
It always protects, always trusts,
always hopes, always perseveres."

1 Corinthians 13:6-7
New International Version (NIV)

October 13

It's been exactly 7 years and 6 months today, since Maxwell's passing and I miss him so much. I never got a chance to thank him for showing me how a woman should be treated.

As you know, James was convicted and sentenced to life in prison without parole. I also heard that, Nee and China finally got married and now have twins, Asiah and Affrika. Poor Nee, I know it must be difficult living in a house with all those women. And China needs to be smacked, she has that man in the house with all those foreign countries.....what's next? They get a dog named it Russia?

I heard Bruce got to James before the police. It's been said that, "Two wrongs don't make things right." but to me it does. Just knowing for a few moments, he felt that same pain that Maxwell felt is just as satisfying. They say James may never walk again, which is fine with me. It pleases me, to know that he can't run when they try to take his ass in prison. Hell, I can't lie it makes me feel damn good inside.

Speaking of Bruce, a little birdie told me that you and Bruce are expecting. Oh Lord, that means I have to shop around to find a baby rattle that's shape like a 9mm. (Ha-ha!) Congrats to you two!

As for me, I'm doing well. I'm loving it here is Arizona I think that leaving DC and the east coast completely was the best thing I ever did. The commission from the Vanderbilt's sale and purchase along with my competitor offering to buy me out has a sista sitting kinda right. I had the grand opening of my bakery last week and it's doing well.

Girl, you would be surprised at some of the requests I get for custom made cakes. I get weird request for cakes shaped like private body parts and hand expressions like someone's middle finger. Yep, you read it right, this guy caught his wife cheating so; he wanted to send her a cake of his middle finger. The weird thing was he called to switch it with his daughter's Dora the Explorer birthday cake. So, you can imagine the reaction he got, when he showed up with that cake.

On another note, I have been spending a lot of time soul searching, trying to find out who I am, and where I am in life. I have come to realize, it's not a man that completes you. You complete yourself. I wasted a lot of time, thinking that, having the right man in my life would make me all the things I wanted to be. I understand now, what you meant when you said, "A man is an accessory and not a necessity."

Happiness, self-respected, self-esteem and pride are God given treasures, that everyone women has inside and no man, not Nehemiah, Bruce ,James and even Maxwell can give or take away from you. I think it was Bill Clinton who said, "You can't take away things that you did not give."

As for now, I am happy just doing the "Me thing." Will I ever find love again? Maybe, but if I do, It will be solely because I choose to be with him and not because I need him.

Well, I will end here, take care of yourself Bruce and my little niece or nephew send pictures....a lot (LoL). Give China and Nee my love and let her know that this sista over her is going to be fine.

Love,
Christina

(Here is a sample of my next novel.)

One Size, Does Not Fit All

"Man, I can't believe that I am here." Kaliq disgustedly said to himself as he sat impatiently waiting. He glanced around the room, looking at the walls adorned with countless diplomas and citations from prestigious schools like Princeton, Yale, even Harvard.

"I bet this dude is one of those overly educated, faded khakis dressing, seven days a week tweed blazer sporting, brown loafers and white socks wearing geek who probably got punked in school on the regular for his lunch money."

He continuously shifted his body from one position to the next fidgeting like a child during a long Sunday morning church sermon.

"Yeah, I think that everybody had at least one in their class. When I was in high school, they used to play Dungeons and Dragons during lunch and even had parties just to play that silly game. I bet he's one of those people that have a lot of book smarts and not a lick of common sense. The type that tells those corny intellectual jokes that only bookworms like him can understand or even thinks is funny."

Then he quickly jumped to his feet and began pacing, "Man, I got to figure out a way to get out of this. Maybe, I won't say too much and he'll see that I'm fine then I can go home. I shouldn't have let Carlows (Carlos) talk me into coming here. This is his doctor and not mine, I don't need any help, and in fact, I feel just as fine as I look. Damn, I wish this Dr. A. Larrieux would hurry up; I don't have all day to be sitting around having some dork pick and probe me. Hmm, I wonder what the "A" stands for and what kinda name is Larrieux anyway? Huh, the "A" probably stands for Albert or Alvin. No, it stands for Archibald. What a loser!"

Just then, Dr. Larrieux walked in and corrected him, "Actually Mr. Lovelace, its Dr. A.A. Larrieux, Alexis Angelica Larrieux. In addition, the name Larrieux is Franco-American, French; I am a descendant of a long bloodline of Acadians. Yet, because our skin is so light, most of us can past for Caucasian and African-American so, we are commonly referred to as Creole and sometimes Cajuns."

Kaliq turned around and to his surprise there stood the voluptuous Dr. Larrieux, nothing at all what he expected. His eyes lit up as he peered up at her amazing Amazonian 6 foot even, 200-pound stature, which towered over him like the Greek Goddess of Love, Aphrodite.

She looked down at him as though she were looking down from the heavens. Her perfume seemed to secrete stealthily from her body. Her scent Rumba danced its way over to where he sat robbing his mind of every single thought he had that second, that minute and even that day.

"I thought Cajuns were white folks that live in the swamp?" he stutters.

She politely answers, "No that is a common misconception; although some do choose to live in rural areas. The word Creole actually means "home grown, not imported," referring to the fact that my family, both whites and blacks were born in the French colony of Louisiana. It commonly refers to the French-speaking black culture and the dialect of French we speak in Louisiana."

Rather than to continue to sit there dumbfounded, Kaliq said the first thing off the top of his head, "So you're from Louisiana, huh?" Then mentally kicking himself, "Smooth move Kaliq, real smooth. You idiot didn't she just tell you that?"

She continued to enter her office and sits down in the chair next to his, "Yes, born and raised on Etouffée, Jambalaya and King Cake. But that's not important, Mr. Lovelace, what brings you into my office today?"

The fluctuation of his voice, as he answered was a dead give-away that he was just as nervous about being there as a death row inmate on execution day.

When he spoke, his voice was high pitched at first, then cracked before returning to normal, "Well my friend Carlos is one of your patients, and he said you were real cool and that I should come in to meet with you."

"So you went through all the trouble of making an appointment just so you could meet me?"

"Ah yeah."

"Including going through all the trouble of getting a referral and coverage verification, just so you could meet me? Don't you think that is a little extreme? As if meeting over coffee was not an option."

"Yes, I mean no!

"Mr. Lovelace, Did your friend Carlos, tell you what type of a doctor I am?"

www.ingramcontent.com/pod-product-compliance
Lightning Source LLC
Chambersburg PA
CBHW070329260626
47160CB00003B/989